Engineering Stories

Short Stories (Realistic Fiction) in Science, Technology, Engineering, and Math (STEM)

Come into my office, conference room, and laboratory - Experience my adventures, teams, challenges, thoughts, travels, and sudden insights

Kenneth Richard Hardman

D1617516

This book is a work of fiction. The characters, incidents, and dialogue are drawn from the author's imagination. Any resemblance to specific events or persons, living or dead, is coincidental.

ISBN: 1483949869
ISBN-13: 978-1483949864

Illustration Credits
Cover Pin Mold with Foot Shape, photo by Jaren Wilkey of BYU Photo, Used with Permission. The Orbital Mechanic, illustration by Lisa Anne Hardman. Unless otherwise noted, all other photos or illustrations by the author.

DEDICATION

Glenn and Dorothy Hardman

To My Father and Mother, for teaching me, no, for showing me how to work, how to play, how to smile, and how to care.

CONTENTS

1 - GET A GRIP 1

2 - THE ORBITAL MECHANIC 45

3 - FOOT NOTES 61

4 - QUICK STEP 81

5 - CUTTING EDGE - A CAPSTONE PRIMER 109

    Part 1 - Meet the Team 109

    Part 2 - Meet the Customer 114

    Part 3 - Experience The Product 120

    Part 4 - Uncover Customer Needs 124

    Part 5 - Refine the Specifications 129

    Part 6 - Compose the Functions 133

    Part 7 - Go Benchmarking 139

    Part 8 - Sketch Many Concepts 143

    Part 9 - Explain and Discuss Concepts 146

    Part 10 - Architect the Machine 151

    Part 11 - Rate, Rank, and Score............................156

    Part 12 - Build Prototypes 160

    Part 13 - Conduct your Design Review...................161

    Part 14 - Design all the Details..............................168

    Part 15 - Collaborate and Solve 171

    Part 16 - Purchase, Fabricate, Assemble...............175

    Part 17 - Test and Refine.......................................178

    Part 18 - Deliver, Install, Demonstrate..................184

6 - SPEED READER 187

7 - THE RIBBON CUTTING 205

8 - MY JOURNEY TO ENGINEERING............................231

SYNOPSIS OF EACH STORY...242

ABOUT THE AUTHOR 244

PREFACE

Engineering Stories are Realistic Fiction, short story dramatizations allowing the reader, through narration, description, dialogue, and thought to experience the challenges and satisfaction of being an engineer, inventor, or scientist. Stories are very plausible, being a composition of author experience and the experiences of his peers. Herein, the reader is able to listen into the minds of engineers, see how they think, observe how they might behave, understand what makes them tick. The objective is to encourage students to consider or continue careers in science, technology, engineering, or math (STEM), show what it may be like, dispel a myth or two, and encourage creativity, problem solving, and the confidence to make the world a better place.

Engineering has been a good profession for me. Growing up, I didn't know what engineering was. I knew that my grandfather was a machinist in the aerospace industry, and that my father used machines in his cabinet making work, but I didn't know who designed and made the machines. Working in my father's shop, I was good at making wood products, but I was much more fascinated by the machines, than the furniture.

In my first serious semester of college, I toured the university talking to professors, asking about careers in communications, construction, industrial design, and engineering. As soon as I learned what engineers do, I knew it was for me. Mechanical Engineering was described to me as the activity of converting energy from one form to another, converting raw materials into useful products, and solving problems to make the world a better place; I was excited.

On more that one occasion through my life I have heard the troubling phrase, "I hate math!" This pronouncement or plea usually came from youth, and sometimes would be followed by, "I could never be an engineer." Considering most of the kids I have met, I don't believe either of these claims. I believe that a youth comes to hate math because they got behind in their understanding of math principles and processes, sat in frustration in their school desk or in tears around the dining room table because their teacher, day after day, was moving on whether they understood it or not. Often, the student's parents were not able to help. This sequence of events led the student to give up on math exclaiming, "What am I ever going to use this for anyway."

Engineering Stories is not a math book, but it is my attempt to give the wondering student application for math and science, and the wandering student vision to see what it may be like to be an engineer or technologist. In my opinion, professionals should give something in return for what they have received in their career. Engineering Stories is my attempt to give something back to youth who deserve opportunities to live life fully, and make satisfying contributions to the world. I encourage all professionals to do the same.

If there is anything selfish in the creation of this book, it is my desire to learn, in this case, learn how to write better. Can you believe it, an engineer who wants to write better? Throughout my career I have met many engineers and students who do not like to write, and yet writing is one of the fundamental communication methods we have to convey our ideas and designs. Perhaps one of these stories will encourage one youth or engineering student somewhere in the world to think more favorably about writing.

Another powerful communication method is drawing, illustrating, or sketching. It has been my observation that the person in the conference room or cubicle who can sketch their thinking is the one who drives or moves the project forward. Sketch! Even if you don't think you can. Learn. Continue to learn. Don't be afraid to learn.

Seven realistic stories are included in this volume. They are fictionalized compositions based on a lifetime of career experiences. The focus in this volume is engineering product development which involves the activities of developing a product to satisfy the needs and desires of a customer. The customer could be a company, a work group, or an individual. The product could be a method of transportation, fabrication, or medical utility. These stories illustrate how customer needs are gathered, how product requirements are refined, and how creativity is used to determine good potential solutions to the product requirements. Examples are included showing the process by which options are evaluated, selected, designed, built, tested, and put to work for the customer.

Like any good story, Engineering Stories show character development, how individuals work on their own and in teams to tackle challenges and build better products. Engineers travel, engineers learn, engineers struggle, engineers grow, and engineers feel joy in what they accomplish.

This book can be used as supplemental material for the classroom. At the end of each story, mentor notes and exercises have been included to emphasize engineering ideas and encourage critical thinking, a very important engineering quality. The teacher is encouraged to assign this material to the student or use these questions for class discussion, and the student is encouraged to write responses to the questions.

Finally, enjoy these stories. Encourage others to read them. If you can relate to these protagonists, these engineers, and find yourself improving upon what they have done, then you are probably an engineer, or should be.

ACKNOWLEDGMENTS

Many have provided encouragement and peer review for these stories. I express appreciation to directors, coaches, staff, and students of the Brigham Young University Department of Mechanical Engineering Capstone program. Specifically, I wish to thank Dr. Robert Todd for endless encouragement, and Dr. Carl Sorensen for honest and significant story critique. I am grateful to Braden Hancock, junior in Mechanical Engineering for his student perspective and expertise in english helping to improve the manuscript. I acknowledge and thank my mentor and friend Timothy Bridges for his generous encouragement and belief in my purpose and capability. I acknowledge and thank my encouraging and supportive wife and children for being proud of the engineer in their lives.

ENGINEERING STORIES

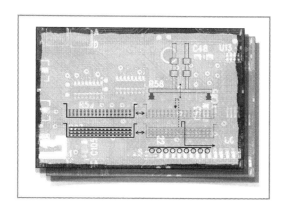

1 - GET A GRIP

"Okay everyone, listen-up." Brandon leaned forward bringing the Monday morning staff meeting to attention. "The rumors are true."

"Oh no." Melissa thought, arms crossed, hands gripping her upper arms. "Was everyone against hiring me?"

Brandon, middle-aged with brown hair, was the engineering manager at International Custom Automation (ICA), reputable creators of special robotic machines. Each Monday, the Automation Group met in a small conference room on the third floor.

"The good news is," Brandon continued, "the board of directors approved launching their new smart phone to compete with the latest technology."

Melissa relaxed her hands into her lap.

"The bad news; the new phone must hit the market in ten months; we have eight months to develop, test, and install new automation at LIC (Long Island Circuits) in New York for the printed circuit board (PCB) processing line."

"Cool." Melissa sat against the wall thinking. "My first week on the job and there's a major announcement." For a moment, her eyes wandered to the window overlooking part of Jersey City. She could see the Statue of Liberty, the Hudson, and the Manhattan skyline.

Mike, another engineer asked. "Is this automation for the inner layers, or rigid PCBs?"

Brandon responded while glancing from Mike over to Melissa. "Our machine will feed inner-layer cores into the DES line."

"DES line?" Melissa moved her lips without speaking.

Brandon paused. "Before we go any further, let's welcome our newest engineer to ICA, Melissa Stewart."

Melissa raised her hand slowly, head tilted down slightly. The seven other engineers in the room nodded in her direction.

"Aaron?" Brandon addressed a thin haired older man, white shirt, no tie, sitting near the head of the conference table. "Melissa came to us top in her class, but there's a lot of terminology she'll need to know about printed circuit boards, and the kind of automation we develop."

Aaron rubbed the back of his neck.

Turning to the corner of the room Brandon continued. "Melissa, go ahead and take notes, but please ask Aaron anything you don't understand. Don't wait till later, go ahead and ask him during the meeting if you like, or any time."

Aaron looked over his glasses and nodded to Melissa.

"Okay, let's get started. Here's what we know so far about the automation we need to design. The final circuit board inside each phone will be two inches wide by three and a half inches tall; about two millimeters thick. Each board will be cut from panels about two feet square, twelve layers thick."

Melissa made notes in her crisp new company notebook pretending to understand what Brandon was talking about.

Aaron looked preoccupied, then interrupted, "Brandon?" Aaron tapped his fingers on his well used, dog-eared notebook.

"Yah Aaron."

"Could we take a few minutes right now and get some of these fundamental terms out for Melissa? I may not have time later, and I can see already she's scratch'n her head."

"Sure." Brandon looked at his watch, then at the whiteboard. "Aaron, why don't you give us all a review. This'll be good for everyone. We'll listen while you explain it to Melissa."

"Okay." Aaron got up slowly, walked to the

whiteboard and carefully drew a matrix, a rectangular array of horizontal and vertical lines, with a border around the whole thing.

"It looks like a checkerboard." Melissa thought.

Looking around the room Aaron said. "Everyone hold up your cell phone. Inside every phone, smart phone, e-book reader, and just about every electronic device you can think of is a printed circuit board. I'll just call it a PCB. It's made of laminations of many layers of thin copper, each layer separated by non-conducting layers." Aaron placed his cell phone on the table and pulled from his notebook a picture of a circuit board with shiny copper traces, like a labyrinth trail separated by faded green material.

"This seems kind'a fundamental." Melissa thought. "I learned about PCBs in EE 101."[1]

"The copper traces provide electrical pathways between components that will be mounted later on the board like memory chips, resisters, touch screens, keyboards, and capacitors. Having multiple layers allows the product to have many combinations of circuit pathways or traces in a small package. Melissa, hold up your cell phone."

Melissa did so.

"Looks like you could use a new one." Aaron said.

Brandon leaned forward and inserted. "I'll have a comment about that in a minute."

---

[1] The acronym EE is short for Electrical Engineering. 101 is usually a fundamental class catalog number at a university.

Aaron raised an eyebrow and continued. "The circuit board in your device may be a few square inches in surface area." Aaron pointed at the picture again. "When manufactured, these circuit boards were fabricated one core, or layer, at a time in large sheets, four to six square feet, laminated to create a muti-layer board or panel of 2 to 30 layers then cut into the final size like cutting brownies from a cookie sheet into small pieces to be populated with components, then packaged in your phone."

Aaron lifted the edge of a page of his notebook with his thumb and let it flip back down. "Before lamination, each core is very thin, paper thin, and very flexible. While in this state, each core has a pattern of copper traces photographically exposed on it and then the unwanted copper is chemically removed in an etching process. In this way, very large quantities of small electrical pathways can be created. These thin flexible cores must be taken from trays and placed onto the chemical conveyor, then after etching away the unwanted copper, they must be lifted from the conveyor and stacked while waiting for the next process. They must be handled with care causing no damage to the base material, the copper traces, or any other features on the core or it must be scrapped. If damage is not detected until after later steps, like lamination, and de-panalization, then the cost of scrap is high."

Aaron's phone rang. He retrieved it from the table and looked at the phone's screen. He turned to Brandon and said, "It's our customer. Should I..."

"Take the call," Brandon insisted. "They are as anxious as we are to get started."

"Yes, this is Aaron." Everyone listened while Aaron spoke to his phone. "Yes I have that information at my desk." Aaron looked out the window. "Oh, really?" "Let me get to my office ... hold on." Aaron looked at Brandon.

"Go. Go." Brandon said to Aaron. "I'll take over from here."

Aaron grabbed his notebook and left.

Brandon continued the lecture. "Each inner layer core starts with a full thin layer of copper on the surface, then it's coated with a material that's resists or blocks light called photoresist. The photoresist coating is exposed with a circuit image using a special optical projector, then the unwanted copper is etched away in a chemical bath; that's what they call DES, or develop, etch, strip. The photoresist is developed, the copper is etched, and the photoresist is stripped off. That's where we come in; we need to create a machine, a robot that will take each exposed layer from a tray and place them one at a time onto the chemical process conveyor, and then at the other end of the chemical process, we need a similar machine to lift each developed core off the conveyor and place them into another tray for further processing and inspection."

Melissa rubbed her nose. "I think I understand."

"Okay." Brandon said. "So, each core is about two foot square. One of our machines will pick it from a tray before copper etching, the other machine will pick it from the conveyor with much of the copper removed and place it in a tray. Typically we use vacuum cups to grip panels and lift them, but these new technology cores are so thin, there is some concern that the vacuum cups will wrinkle, peel, or damage the copper traces."

"You were going to say something about Melissa's cell phone." Mike asked.

"Oh yah. ICA plans to give each member of the team a new smart phone on the first day they hit the market..."

Each person in the room sat up in their chairs.

"If we make the deadline." Brandon clarified. "And ICA is going to pay for each data plan for two years, maybe longer."

"Double cool—finally, a smart phone." Melissa thought, having been a poor college student.

Brandon handed a small stack of papers to Mike and asked him to pass them around.

"Okay." Brandon said looking in the direction of Mike and Melissa. "I'm assigning Mike, Aaron, and Melissa to develop the overall PCB handling and gripping machine architecture."

Melissa opened her eyes wide.

Brandon continued. "This project is similar to past panel handlers we've done so I would like the core team, the rest of you to develop the main structure, electrical, and safety features. The software team will do what they do best. In one week, we will have a high level system review to go over the main functions and see some initial ideas from the gripping team. Okay everyone, study what I just gave you and get to work on your subsystems."

The meeting adjourned.

Mike introduced himself to Melissa. "Welcome. Here, I'll show you where Aaron's office is. I think he'll be waiting for us."

Mike and Melissa made their way from one corner of the third floor to another passing rows of cubicles, the lunch room, and the water cooler.

"Why did Brandon choose me?" Melissa held one palm up while holding her notebook in the other hand. "Isn't the gripping part of the machine the most technically challenging? I mean, I'm excited at the opportunity, but I thought it would take some time before I..."

"Oh Brandon is like that." Mike replied. "He's pretty smart, actually, putting the newest person together with the most experienced engineer like Aaron. It's a good way to pass on knowledge. The others don't mind too much because everyone gets opportunities to work on different parts of the machine. Besides, some of the other team members are skilled doing the electrical, or the structure, or software. Maybe you have some particular skill Brandon thinks will be needed on this project."

Melissa thought about her resume and job interview with Brandon four weeks ago. "I don't have any experience with printed circuit board handling. I wonder what Brandon is thinking..."

"Hey, get in here you two." Aaron was waiting at the

door of his office and rushed them inside. "That was our big client on the phone. How soon can you guys be ready for a trip to Israel?"

Melissa dropped her jaw.

Mike got his words out first. "Are you serious? How soon do they need us?"

"Well, Brandon was serious; this is a huge deal for LIC and they are ready to lay out their factory process and determine what kind of machines and floor space are needed for the chemical process lines. They would like us there tomorrow, but a day later is probably the best we can do."

"I thought the client was in New York?" Melissa asked.

"They are." Aaron said. "But as it turns out, the printed circuit board layers that we need to handle are similar to some prototype boards being made by their branch in Israel. LIC wants us there to learn some specifics about the process and develop a concept for our machines."

"I can't believe it." Melissa said under her breath.

"Melissa, is this going to be a problem for you?"

"No, not at all. Actually it's exciting. I just didn't think things would happen so fast."

"Actually," Mike said. "I know for a fact that Brandon wanted you here sooner, but it took a while for Human Resources to get your job offer ready..."

"Well," Aaron said. "I've got our travel department ready to make reservations as soon as we tell them the time. I was planning on having a brainstorm session in my office today but that will have to wait 'till we are on the plane. In the mean time, get your... Oh wait, Melissa, do you have a Passport?"

"Yes, I got one a couple years ago when I..."

"Oh good. So, get your personal information to me in the next hour and I'll work with travel to get us all sitting next to each other on the plane so we can go over these requirements." Aaron held up the sheet of paper distributed in the conference room.

A day later, 3:30 in the afternoon, Melissa arrived at the El Al Airlines departure gate at Newark, their Jumbo jet filling the window. The gate sign read, "Flight 52 to Tel Aviv Departing at 4:45 p.m."[2]

"Good afternoon Melissa." Mike said. "Have you seen Aaron yet?"

"Not yet but I can't imagine our leader being late."

"Well, it's happened before." Mike said with a small snicker. "Sometimes at work he gets pretty preoccupied thinking deeply and..."

"Hello Mike. Hi Melissa." Aaron said, a little out of breath. "Hey did each of you bring your notebooks, or..."

"Yah, I've got mine." Melissa patted a flat spot on her carry-on bag.

"Yep, I'm ready." Mike added. "Aaron, last time I flew across the Atlantic, I remember not getting enough sleep on the plane and I was seriously lagged for a

---

[2] Tel Aviv is a major city in Israel

couple days. I'm thinking we should start our discussion early in the flight so we can close our eyes for the last few hours."

"Yah, you're right." Aaron said looking around the gate seating area. "Actually, we don't board for another thirty minutes, shall we get started? There are a few seats over there in the corner." Aaron pointed.

"I need to use the restroom." Mike said. "I'll join you in a couple minutes."

"Okay." Aaron pulled out the specification sheet Brandon provided. "On my way out of the office, Brandon told me that the inner layers, or cores will be one mil thick (that's one-thousandth of an inch) and separated by slip-sheets to protect the photoresist."

"I remember about the inner-layers and photoresist," Melissa said, "but what's a slip-sheet?"

"It's just a piece of paper interleaved between each core to protect the photoresist coating while stacked in the tray. The challenge is, our machine must detect the top item in the tray and determine whether it's an inner layer or a slip-sheet. If it's a slip sheet, then our machine needs to remove it and place it in a stack somewhere, and if it's a inner layer, then our machine needs to place it on the DES conveyor."

Melissa understood, then sat back in her chair.

"We've done this before so it shouldn't be a problem. It just makes our machine bigger because we have to have a tray for PCBs and a separate tray for..."

"Aaron." Melissa interrupted. "I'm still stunned at being put on this team my first week of work; first day actually. Why did Brandon choose me for this assignment?"

"Well," Aaron paused sitting back. "I know of three reasons."

"Three?" Melissa gave Aaron her full attention.

"First, some of us won't be around forever and senior management is putting a lot of pressure to get us to teach the new engineers all we can."

Melissa nodded understandingly.

"Second," Aaron squinted, "actually the second reason is because I asked for you specifically to be on this team."

"You did? Why?"

"Because on your senior project in college, you had experience working with compressible flow and with small membrane or thin film mechanics. When I saw those two skills together, I knew we needed you on the gripping team. As PCB technology advances and the layers get thinner and thinner, we need to consider them as thin membranes. We are approaching the edge of our technology gripping these sheets with vacuum cups."

"I see." Melissa said.

"Well, I sure think your expertise will help as time goes on," Aaron added.

"Thanks, I think." Melissa said scratching her neck. "That makes me feel nervous, and useful at the same time."

"Join the crowd." Aaron said as he looked back at his notes. "Now, where were we?"

"You said there were three reasons."

"Oh yah. We noticed from your interview portfolio that you have good drawing and presentation skills. Most of the young engineers don't learn how to sketch anymore and communicate their ideas with free hand or technical drawing. It looks like you made the effort to develop this skill. You'll find it to be a powerful asset in your career."[3]

Melissa thought back to her senior project. "Thanks. I'll do my best."

"Now, where were we?"

"Oh yes, Brandon also said that this DES line is a little longer than most so there won't be a lot of room at each end of the line for our automation."

"There's never enough floor space." Mike overheard Aaron as he approached from behind then sat down and drew a sketch of the DES line with material handling automation at each end.

"When the PCBs come off the other end of the line," Melissa pointed at Mikes sketch, "do they need to be re-stacked with slip-sheets?"

Aaron's face wrinkled. "I'm not sure, Brandon wasn't clear on that. I'll call him while we board the plane."

Melissa opened her notebook and drew something

---

[3] "Technical sketching is used as a means of rapid graphical communication that enables the engineer to quickly express, explain, and record her or his ideas." Dale H. Besterfield, Robert E. O'Hagan, *Technical Sketching with an Introduction to CAD For Engineers, Technologists, and Technicians. 3rd Edition.*

similar to what she saw in Mike's book.

"What are the rest of the specifications and constraints?" Mike asked.

"Just the ones on the sheet." Aaron replied. "Melissa, why don't you read it out loud for us and let's discuss it."

"DES Inner-Layers: Panel size: 24 by 24 inches. Panel thickness: 1 mil. Panel material: Glass reinforced epoxy dielectric core coated with copper and dry film photoresist. Panel surface properties: Full copper before DES; Copper traces after DES."

"Oh I forgot." Aaron reached into his travel bag. "Here's a sample." He handed a business card sized piece of inner-layer core to Melissa.

Melissa flexed it between her thumb and forefinger then handed it to Mike. "It really is like a piece of paper."

"Please continue." Aaron said nodding at the specification sheet.

"Maximum tray stacking depth: two inches. Slip-sheeting material: To Be Determined."

"What does that mean?" Melissa asked.

Mike responded. "It means that when this was written, they hadn't chosen the type of paper yet."

"Well," Aaron said. "Now we know from Brandon that there will indeed be slip-sheets between each core."

Melissa continued. "Feeder: A means to remove panels from a tray one at a time and place them on a conveyor adjacent to the tray. One core must be placed on the conveyor every eight seconds continuously 24/7

(30 minutes allowable downtime per day for maintenance). Receiver: A means to remove one panel at a time from the conveyor placing it in an adjacent tray."

Mike handed the sample back to Aaron. "One way to approach this is to consider the 'material path' options. I did a little thinking on this last night."

"Great." Aaron said. "I have some thoughts on it as well. Mike, go ahead and get us started. For now I suggest we each keep notes in our individual lab books and later, perhaps when we get there, we can combine our ideas."

The waiting area was filling in.

Mike sat between Aaron and Melissa, pointing at notes and sketches in his notebook and began. "For the Feeder, each sheet, whether core or slip-sheet, starts from a horizontal position in the tray but at a progressively lowering elevation as the stack is depleted. In this first concept, the vacuum grippers lower until they touch the top item in the tray. Vacuum cups are all around the perimeter of the panel avoiding the exposed area to be etched. The vacuum is energized, gripping the top item and raising it a couple inches to clear the height of the rim of the tray. I didn't know about the slip-sheet requirement when I drew these last night, but in each case, there needs to be a sensor of some kind to determine if the top panel is a slip-sheet or an inner-layer core. Again, in this first concept, if the top layer is a core, it moves horizontally toward the conveyor, then it is lowered and released onto the conveyor."

"Suppose," Aaron said rubbing his chin pointing his pencil at Mike's sketch. "Suppose if the top piece is a slip-sheet, then it moves in the opposite direction, away from the conveyor over a slip-sheet tray, is lowered and released into another tray."

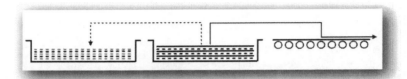

"I see where you're going with this." Melissa bravely added. "With this concept, the platform holding the vacuum grippers would have three stations, one over each of the two trays, and one over the conveyor." Now Melissa was pointing at Mike's drawing. "It would essentially pick a panel from the main tray in the middle and alternately place one to the left and one to the right."

"But what if for some reason," Aaron said, testing Melissa, "there are two slip-sheets in a row, one on top of the other?"

"A sensor or camera would have to detect that condition so the controller can take the right action." Melissa clutched her pencil tightly.

"Excellent." Aaron acknowledged. "Mike, I see you have some more concepts."

"The second option is similar to the first, except cores are not lifted from all four sides around the panel, they are lifted by the leading edge and dragged onto the conveyor. There would need to be a set of vacuum grippers for the slip-sheets to be dragged one direction and a set of grippers for the cores to be dragged in the other direction."

"Can we do that?" Melissa squinted and looked up at Aaron.

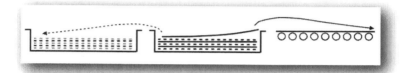

"Probably not." Aaron said. "But Mike is pretty good at generating a lot of concepts, even ones that don't pan out, but usually we learn something from each one."

Melissa nodded.

"This next concept is not very practical, but I think we should include it. The inner-layer core edge farthest from the conveyor is gripped and elevated high above the tray passing over the other edge flipping the sheet over and lowering it onto the conveyor. It's like the dragging option but the panel gets flipped over."

"Hmm." Melissa thought. "That looks risky."

Mike looked up at Aaron for a second, then over to Melissa then continued.

"Now this next option is like the first, except the leading-edge of the panel gets swapped. The horizontal sheet is raised vertically from the tray as before, then pivoted 180 degrees about a vertical axis to the side of the tray and the conveyor, then lowered onto the conveyor. I don't see any big advantage here, it just allows for a different type of translation of the panel; option one uses linear motion to move the gripper assembly, and this option uses rotational motion."

"Very creative." Aaron said.

"You're good at this." Melissa said to Mike.

"Well, that's what I have so far."

Aaron adjusted his posture then held his open notebook in front of Mike. "What do you think of this option?" Suppose our machine hangs over the end of the chemical DES conveyor such that our inner-layer tray is installed by the operator into a compartment directly over the end of the conveyor. Then, like your first option Mike, the gripping head raises the top panel up out of the tray, and then, instead of moving the gripping assembly and core horizontally, it's the tray that is moved horizontally away from the conveyor, then the gripping head lowers the panel all the way down onto the conveyor for release. The head then raises back up and then the tray returns horizontally to the starting position."

"That's good thinking." Mike said. "That kind of configuration could save floor space."

"But what if the top piece is a slip-sheet?" Melissa asked.

"Well," Aaron thought for a moment. "If you combine this concept with the one that drags the slip sheet out of the way, then maybe it'll work."

"Yah." Mike added. "If the top piece is a slip-sheet, then the main gripping head doesn't pick it up, a secondary vacuum bar reaches in and pulls the slip-sheet out to a compartment below or above the tray elevation."

"Why not have two trays above the conveyor?" Melissa blurted out.

Aaron and Mike turned to Melissa for an explanation.

"Suppose the gripping head has enough vertical travel to access panels at three elevations, the conveyor, the main core or slip-sheet tray, and one even higher, the slip-sheet only tray." Melissa sketched the concept in her notebook showing Mike and Aaron the details of her thought."

"I see what you're talking about." Aaron said.

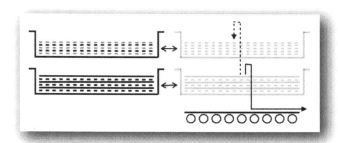

"This way, there is no separate slip-sheet gripper. There is only one set of grippers and it only has to travel up and down. The trays are the only things that move horizontally."

"I'm impressed." Mike said.

"I see what you mean by ideas building on each other." Melissa remembered.

"Melissa." Aaron asked. "Do you have any other ideas?"

"Well, I was thinking of copy machines and printers. A ream of paper is loaded into a compartment, then some rubber rollers drag or grip the top piece and send it through rollers and guides through the process." Melissa looked up to see the response from Aaron and Mike. "Well, I guess it isn't a good idea because the rollers could damage..."

"Wait." Mike said. "Let the ideas flow freely, even ideas that seem unrealistic or potentially bad."

"That's right." Aaron added. "Like the dragging grippers, experience tells me that part of every concept could be useful. Keep thinking like that..."

"Good afternoon passengers." A voice over the airport speakers interrupted their discussion. "This is a pre-boarding announcement for flight 52 to Tel Aviv. We are now inviting those passengers with small children, and any passengers requiring special assistance, to begin boarding..."

"I guess we'd better get ready to board. This has been a great start."

After boarding the aircraft, seated in the center seats of coach class, Aaron, Mike and Melissa listened to the inflight safety briefing, then continued their discussion.

The tight working space, meal interruptions, and flight noise prevented open and free conversation but with the use of sketches, they developed a few more concepts and began evaluating the pros and cons of each. Four hours into the eleven-hour and twenty-two minute flight, they began to wind down. After an in-flight movie, most of the passengers, including Mike and Aaron were asleep. Melissa couldn't sleep; this was here first trip over the Atlantic.

The flight was smooth, except for some turbulence descending over the Mediterranean and into Tel Aviv. At the baggage claim, each explained why they were visiting the country and then met their driver at the curb. When asked what the purpose of her trip was, Melissa pulled up a blank for a second—she had been so busy being fascinated by the flight, the plane, and the new destination. During the car ride from Ben Gurion International Airport to LIC-Asia on the north west corner of Tel Aviv, her face was against the window as she examined the people, the buildings, and the markets.

"Hello, My name is Gad Shalev. Aaron, it is good to see you again. Thank you for coming on such short notice."

Introductions were made and Mike, Melissa and Aaron received a tour of the facility before going to a conference room for discussions with several PCB process specialists. It was 2:00 p.m. local time on Wednesday and Melissa was beginning to drag from the jet lag and loss of sleep, but she had been encouraged to stay awake until it was time to sleep locally. The group did not have as much time as they hoped, to compile all their notes.

"Okay," Gad began the conference room discussion. In the center of the table was a bowl of oranges, tangerines and pomelit, and a dish of flatbread and hummus. "We know you are tired and probably hungry, but, actually, we are all tired as well. The new smart phone announcement and aggressive time schedule has taken us by surprise and we are working hard to develop our chemical process concepts for all of our process lines. I think we should get right to it. Please help yourself to some fresh fruit and flatbread."

"We have come with a few potential automation concepts." Aaron opened his notebook and pulled out the specification sheet provided by Brandon and handed it to Gad. "Gad, would you please review this spec' sheet and tell us if it is the latest revision? We understand we will be focusing on the Feeder and Receiver for the new DES Line."

Gad scanned down the list of requirements. "Actually, this looks pretty good except we are not certain of the feed rate, or panels per minute, yet. We are still working out the chemistry and etch rate for these thin cores."

"That's okay." Aaron continued. "Can you describe the physical interface with the feeder and receiver? What does the end of the DES line specifically look like? What is the conveyor height? And how much room will there be at each end for automation?"

Gad removed a rubber band from a large roll of paper and smoothed the sheet out on the table placing books and coffee cups on each corner. It was a layout of the new process line. "Here is the LIC New York facility DES room. There will be three complete DES chemical lines needing three feeders and three receivers." Gad pointed sequentially at three long rows of equipment.

"It looks like we'll be building three of each." Mike said to Aaron.

"Actually," Gad added, "we are hoping that the feeders and receivers are very similar, and..." Gad pointed at another section of the layout. "This is our overflow area. If the product does well on the market, which we all hope it does, then we will add more DES lines here." Gad looked up at the visitors. "We plan to order six feeders and six receivers up front."

Aaron turned to Mike. "I expect we will actually build a total of fourteen machines. The first two will be the prototype feeder and receiver." Aaron then turned to Gad while pointing at the layout on the table. "I see something here that concerns me."

All eyes turned to Aaron and then to the layout where Aaron pointed.

"You show only two and a half meters from the end of each DES line to the wall. How much room do you need for operators and other personnel to walk around the end of each line?"

"A minimum of one meter. The panel carts are 80 centimeters wide."

Melissa did some quick calculations in her head.

"Only one and a half meters for the automation?" Aaron asked with concern. "That's gonna limit our options. We understand that the inner layer cores will arrive at this point with slip-sheets. So we need a machine that will remove the sheets before placing the panel on the conveyor. That usually takes more floor space. Has the DES chemical line design been finalized? Can it be shortened?"

"Like I said," Gad offered, "the line speed hasn't been finalized. Copper etching depth is a function partly of the amount of time the panel stays immersed in the chemicals; the longer the time, the more etching. The DES line has to be longer if we go faster..."

"I understand." Aaron acknowledged. "But with the very thin copper layer, wouldn't that make the etching time shorter?"

"Just in case," Mike spoke up, "we'll have to focus on automation options under one point five meters."

Mike redrew one of the lines in his notebook with a rectangle offset from the line. "Is there room for the automation to extend off to the side of the chemical line? And what are our height constraints?"

Jet-lagged, Melissa yawned and tried to stay connected with the conversation.

The team continued for another half hour, then Aaron suggested they depart, check into their hotel and rise a little early the next day to evaluate concepts and determine ways to develop a machine that can use minimal floor space and still reliably handle the slip-sheets.

"When we return tomorrow," Aaron said to Gad as they walked to the door, "let's look at inner layer core samples and discuss what type of gripping systems will be acceptable."

Thursday morning, the trio from America met in the hotel restaurant a little ragged. With the rush, some had forgotten some personal supplies and electrical adapters for the country. Mike was unshaven and Melissa wasn't able to plug in her hair dryer. During a breakfast of fruits, fish, cheeses, and breads they evaluated the material handling options discussed in route, settled on a likely approach, then returned to LIC and the same conference room.

Gad presented several samples of the inner-layer core material, explaining features and areas of concern. He was very insistent that if the photoresist was damaged by the gripping device, then the panel would not etch correctly and would be scrapped. He also stated that the panels had to be lowered slowly onto the conveyor and that they could not be dropped.

Various details of the feeder and receiver were then discussed considering safety, electrical requirements, operator interaction, and maintenance.

The ICA team then explained their main option for the feeder and receiver configuration, the one where the gripping head places the core directly on the DES conveyor.

"No, no, I don't think that will work." Gad stated. "We have requirements to contain the DES chemical fumes. We always have complete enclosures over our chemical conveyors so there wont be any room for your machine to hang over the end of our machine."

"But in order to have space to put the slip-sheets somewhere," Mike explained, "we need to have two compartments, one for the core tray, and one for the slip-sheets, and I don't think we can do that in one and a half meters of floor space. We have to put our control box and pneumatic panel somewhere."

"I'm sorry," Gad insisted, "but we can only have a small opening on the end of the DES line for the panel to enter. It's the only way we can comply with air cleanliness regulations and protect our operators."

Mike pressed again, "There must be some..."

"Wait, Mike." Aaron interrupted. "We will just have to find a way." Aaron turned to Gad. "We will put our best minds on it and figure out how to fit all the requirements into one and a half meters off the end of the DES equipment. Are there any machine height constraints?"

The meeting continued for a while then after lunch the team met other participants throughout the facility and learned various perspectives on the PCBs, ergonomic requirements, preventative maintenance, and safety regulations. Then by 3:00 p.m. the group was headed south back to the airport along Samuel Street.

Melissa pressed her nose against the window on the right side of the car impressed with the deep blue Mediterranean Sea. They passed a sign that read, Golden Beach. "It's a lot warmer here than at home."

"It's too bad we can't see any historical sites while we're here." Mike said.

"I was thinking the same thing." Melissa added.

"Well," Aaron looked at his watch, thinking a moment. "Our flight is at 6:30. Driver, are there any historical sites on our way to the airport?"

"Oh yes, Jaffa, oldest city in the world. It's the place where Jonah set sail..."

"Is there something we can see in Jaffa and still make our 6:30 flight?" Aaron asked.

"I know just the place." the driver said.

For an hour the group walked quickly and enjoyed archeological sites, old stone buildings, ancient fortifications, a flea market, art galleries, shops, and the Jaffa harbor. Satisfied that they were able to experience at least a sample of the local culture, they returned to the car and on to the airport for the long flight home.

"Welcome back." Brandon greeted Aaron, Mike and Melissa in his office on Friday afternoon in Jersey City. "I know you're dog tired but I need a briefing from you so I can make plans for the team discussion planned for Monday. Good news? Or bad news?"

"Mostly good news." Aaron said looking to Mike and Melissa for confirmation. "There are some constraints that will be difficult to manage, but..." Aaron stopped, thought for a moment then said. "Melissa, why don't you give Brandon a run-down of our trip?"

Melissa took a quick breath, feeling put on the spot, but honored by the opportunity. She began from the discussions in the Newark Airport on Tuesday, and within twenty minutes covered the whiteboard with most of what happened, with a little help here and there from Aaron and Mike.

Brandon listened intently, glancing occasionally to Aaron and Mike with a businesslike smile. "Okay, let's proceed with our system design review on Monday after lunch. Do you think you can have your suggested machine concepts drawn up and illustrated? I'd like to project them on the wall, or post them for all to see while we go through assignments."

"I can do that." Melissa said.

"Thanks Melissa." Aaron said.

"Aaron or Mike," Brandon said, "Could one of you update the specification sheet based on your meeting and make copies for Monday? I'd like to see specific DES interface requirements included."

Melissa went to her desk. "I started work here almost a week ago and haven't spent any time at my desk." Since time was short, she decided to use her artistic skills and hand draw the automation concept instead of using the company computer aided design (CAD) tool. This would allow her to work from home for a couple hours over the weekend.

On Monday, Melissa finished her drawings between staff meeting and the design review and had them scanned so they could be projected.

During the design review, Aaron gave a trip report then explained the updates to the specifications including the limited floor space on each end of the

DES line.

Mike summarized briefly the various concepts that were considered, then Melissa explained the proposed solution that the trio had finalized while on their flight back from Israel.

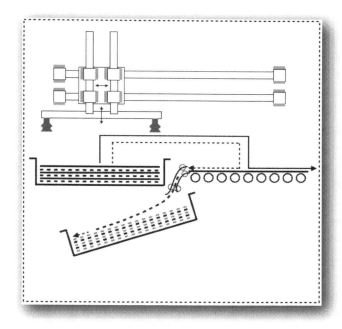

"The machine will sit in line with the DES." Melissa explained pointing at her illustration with one hand and at the facility layout drawing on the table with the other. "There will be two compartments; one right next to the DES line with a conveyor, and one away from the DES line with a tray for the cores and slip-sheets. An overhead gripping assembly will pick up the top sheet, move it over the conveyor, lower it, then release it onto the conveyor. The conveyor will be stopped when a sheet is placed on it. A sensor will detect if the sheet is a core or slip-sheet. If it is a core, then the conveyor will turn on and move the core into the DES to the right. If it is a slip-sheet, then the conveyor will turn in the opposite direction moving the sheet into these slots guiding it under the tray into this slip-sheet stack right here."

After the overview, the three responded to questions from the structures, software, and electrical teams, then action items were given and a rough schedule laid out. While the other groups began making preliminary plans, Melissa was assigned to design and build a prototype gripping head with input from Aaron and Mike. Mike was assigned to design the horizontal and vertical lifting system based on well proven actuator technology. In thirty days, the gripping system would be demonstrated on the samples they brought home, then the final go-ahead would be given for detail design on all the other parts.

For the next few days Melissa performed calculations to determine vacuum cup size and quantity as well as vacuum or suction levels necessary to lift the panels securely, minimizing the chance of dropping a sheet. She studied similar systems, online pneumatic catalogs, and anything else she could find to understand the issues associated with vacuum gripping. She ordered parts and began testing vacuum cups on sample panels.

A few days before the prototype demonstration,

Mike and Melissa put the final prototype hardware together and hooked up the vacuum cups and tubing to a vacuum generator. They made their first attempts on a workbench.

"Wow, it sure grabbed the core." Mike clenched his teeth looking at the core wrinkles on the panel opposite the cup. "I think we'll need to back off on the suction level."

"Do you think it will be a problem?" Melissa asked.

"Remember the thin layer of copper?" Mike said. "We can't buckle it or we might introduce hairline fractures. With your experience with thin membrane theory, you should do some analysis and see what the stress is."

"Okay."

"Also, the buckling might cause the photoresist to peel from the copper, causing etching in the wrong places."

"Oh my." Melissa wiped some sweat from her forehead. "It may take some time to study this thoroughly."

"Well, let me suggest that you get some vacuum cups that have supporting ribs inside. They're pretty common. That should reduce the buckling."

Melissa acquired a pressure regulator and found some rib-reinforced vacuum cups online and got them on order, but she didn't sleep that night. "Fewer cups, larger diameter, lower vacuum level..." She thought through the opposing constraints and decided on the best combination.

The demonstration turned out satisfactory so Brandon gave approval for everyone to move into full scale development. A full CAD model was developed, detail parts and drawings were defined, electrical schematics and functional diagrams were created, and the parts were ordered and fabricated.

Five months into the project the machine was coming together. LIC provided trays, stacks of inner layer cores, and slip-sheets for testing. Excitement was building on the third floor.

"Melissa!" Mike joined Melissa in the machine test laboratory. "Are you ready to show off your stuff?"

"What do you mean? Your horizontal servo slide and vertical pneumatic lifts are the real cool part of this machine."

"Well, I'm pretty excited about them, but it's gonna be nice to finally see some panels moved from the tray onto the conveyor. Shall we load the trays before everyone gets here?"

Mike and Melissa loaded a couple trays alternating cores with slip-sheets then loaded one of the trays into the machine.

Brandon was the last member of his automation group to enter the lab. "Okay everyone, I want to congratulate all of you for your accomplishment, a fully functional machine in just five months. It's time to work out any minor glitches, if any, before the customer preliminary demonstration next week. Aaron, are you guys ready?"

Aaron looked at Melissa and Mike, who nodded.

"Yep. Let's do it." Aaron said.

Mike turned the red emergency stop button and it popped out to the enable position. He then turned the power on and the machine made a few sounds and movements arriving at its 'Ready' state. The green light on top illuminated.

Melissa then pressed the "Cycle" button to start the process.

The gripping head moved horizontally over the tray of cores and slip-sheets, then the vacuum cups descended smoothly into the tray. A hissing sound was heard. The gripping head slowly ascended out of the tray with a core attached nicely to each cup. The core moved horizontally away from the tray over to the conveyor compartment, then it was placed gently on the conveyor and released as the hissing sound stopped. The conveyor moved the panel onto the makeshift DES conveyor. Everyone cheered.

The gripping head then repeated the same motion and descended once again into the tray. A hissing sound was heard. The gripping head slowly ascended out of the tray with...

"Wait!" Someone shouted. "That's not right is it?"

Melissa panicked, bent over looking through the safety glass of the machine at something she had not imagined would happen.

"The vacuum is sucking right through the slip-sheet." Mike said. A slip-sheet and core were attached to most of the vacuum cups. A corner of the core was dangling in midair. "Shall I hit the stop button?"

"Yes," Aaron said. "We don't want to drop the panel and damage these cores if we can help it."

Mike hit the E-Stop[4] which halted all motion and also removed the vacuum. The panel, and slip-sheet dropped from the grippers laying half in the tray and half on the conveyor.

Aaron rubbed his head.

No one spoke; no one knew what to say. Melissa and Mike stared at the machine and at each other. Aaron stayed calm and after a moment began to discuss the problem.

During the next few hours Melissa, Mike, and Aaron ran and reran the machine cycle varying vacuum pressure levels, vacuum cup size and placement on the panels, ascension speed, and any other variable that could be quickly adjusted. They found that if the vacuum suction was too small sometimes the slip-sheet would not stay attached to the cup; if the suction was too large, they would nearly always suck and grip the core right through the slip-sheet. At medium suction, sometimes the machine would only grip the slip-sheet as planned, but sometimes it would suck through and grip the core below. The machine was not at all robust and would not be successful. They certainly could not demonstrate it to their customer this way.

"What if we blow air somehow at the edge of the slip-sheet to get air separation between the paper and

---

4 E-Stop is a common abbreviation for the emergency stop button on machinery and automation.

the core?" Mike suggested.

They tried it but slip-sheets ended up sliding around and sometimes being blown out of the tray. It wasn't pretty.

"What if we reduce the suction level and add some adhesive pads next to the vacuum cups to grip the paper?" Melissa said.

They tried it but after a dozen cycles, the adhesive was depleted and gripping was unsuccessful as before. "Besides, adhesive residue on the photoresist could be a problem during etching." Mike observed.

"What if..." They continued with anything they could think of, but without success.

It was clear that the general solution they had built was not going to work and they would have to start over and do some major rethinking.

"This is so embarrassing." Melissa said hiding the true fact that she was terrified to have such a major failure on her first assignment. Determined, she did some analysis of the physics involved with the interaction between the layers. "How do we induce separation between the two layers while gripping the slip-sheet securely?" she thought. "These guys had a lot of faith in me. Now what am I going to do?"

By now it was late in the evening so everyone went home, down and discouraged.

It was dark, cold and rainy in Jersey City and the chilled humid air penetrated her hoody so she grabbed an extra layer to take a little walk. "Why didn't I think of this problem before?" she thought. "Why didn't Aaron or Mike see this coming? They have years of experience. I was counting on them to keep me from making a fool of myself." She walked along a lighted street between tall buildings shielding her from the wind then into her favorite cafe and sat in the corner. For a moment, she remembered the warm blue Mediterranean.

"Hi Melissa, how's that new job going?" the waitress said. "The other day you were all excited about a big project you were working on."

"Oh, it's going pretty good." Melissa lied, wiping her nose with some tissue. "We had a bit of a challenge today."

"Oh yeh, you look a bit down."

"Could I have a strawberry shake?" Melissa avoided explanation.

"That's not your usual. On a cold night like this I would expect extra rich coffee."

Melissa just looked down at the napkin on the table. The waitress pulled a straw from her apron and laid it beside the napkin then went back to the kitchen.

Melissa picked up the straw, put one end in her mouth and, leaning over put the other end vertical on the flat napkin and breathed in. Slowly raising her head and straw, the napkin rose with the straw.

"Paper is porous." Melissa thought as she slowly reduced the suction until the napkin dropped to the table. She then looked in her wallet, pulled out a business card, and placed it flat on the table with the napkin on top.

Again she picked up the straw, placed it vertically on the napkin and breathed in, a little harder this time. Slowly raising her head and straw, the napkin and business card rose with the straw. "I wonder if they will both drop at the same suction level?" Ever so slowly she reduced the suction and both napkin and card dropped at about the same time. "It takes more flow to keep the napkin gripped. Less flow for the business card. The card is less porous."

The waitress delivered the strawberry shake.

"The porosity is the problem." Melissa said in a quiet voice.

"No one has ever said that about our shakes before."

"Oh, I'm just thinking out loud. Thanks. Could I have another straw please?"

Before putting the other straw into the shake, Melissa put both straws in her mouth, placed the card and napkin on the table such that the card was sticking out from under the napkin enough for one straw to be on the card and the other straw on both the napkin and the card. Melissa sucked and raised her head lifting the layers from the table.

The waitress looked over her shoulder at Melissa.

As she slowly reduced the suction, the straw on the napkin lost grip first. "Air is flowing through the napkin all around the straw and into the straw losing suction and grip. We need paper with less porosity."

Melissa put one of the straws into the shake, then for the next fifteen minutes alternated putting her mouth on each straw as she continued her experiments. She tried tissue, napkins, and even the check from the waitress. The less porous the top layer of paper, the better the probability of gripping the paper and not gripping the card below. "I wonder if our customer would allow us to choose the type or porosity of slip-sheets used in the process?"

Melissa paid the bill then walked to the cafe door. "Where could we get dense paper immediately so we can try it tomorrow, or even tonight?" Melissa pulled out her phone and selected Mike's number.

"Hey Mike, I've been thinking hard on this one and..."

"Yeh, me too. I really think this solution could be made to work if we change the slip-sheet paper. We need heavier bond, less porous paper that won't scratch the photoresist."

Melissa balled her fist, stunned that Mike had taken her thunder, but excited that someone else agreed with her theory.

"Melissa, are you there?"

"Yes, I was just amazed that we were thinking the same thing."

"I'll take that as a compliment." Mike said.

"Where can we get some nonporous paper, large in size and lots of it for our testing?"

"Well," Mike said. "I was just at the department store the other day with my daughter picking up colored poster board for her science display. Let's pick up a stack of posters for starters."

"Good idea." Melissa responded. "I wasn't thinking of paper that thick. I live near the market and I could ask the meat department if I can get a roll of butcher paper. It's thick and coated with some kind of shiny surface. It doesn't leak so it's probably..."

"Excellent." Mike interrupted. "Let's try to get them tonight or at least first thing in the morning so we can cut them to size and run some more cycles."

"I won't be able to sleep. I'm too anxious. Is there any way we could try it tonight?"

When Aaron arrived at the lab the next morning, he found Mike and Melissa running cycles on the new machine. "What's going on?" There were pieces of butcher paper on the floor. "Have you guys been at this all night?"

"Well," Mike said. "After we left last night, some ideas came up and we came back in to give them a try."

Melissa adjusted the straw tucked behind her ear and noticed that Aaron was carrying a large roll of something. "What's that under your arm?"

"I realized last night," Aaron said, "that the machine works fine on cores, without slip-sheets, so we just need a way to have it respond to the slip-sheets in the same way it responds to the cores. Everything needs the same..."

"Porosity?" Mike and Melissa called out in unison.

"Yes." Aaron acknowledged. "So, I remembered a roll of mylar in the old drafting room closet. We haven't used this stuff for years, now that everything is done on

CAD. Anyway, we can cut it into two foot squares and use it as slip-sheets."

"That's what we were thinking."

"Do you think we can persuade our customer to use mylar or heavier paper slip-sheets?" Melissa asked.

"What they care about," Aaron explained, "is that the photoresist on the PCB is protected. If we can demonstrate our machine successfully using one of these materials, I'm certain an appropriate paper or mylar film can be found that will be acceptable to them."

Aaron, Mike, and Melissa spent the next thirty minutes cutting slip-sheets and re-stacking the PCB trays for trials. As they began a machine cycle, Brandon came into the lab along with several others from the automation group.

"Just in time." Aaron said with years of experience behind his confidence. "We'll explain in a minute, but first, watch these next cycles."

It worked perfectly and correctly every cycle. The core went into the DES and the slip-sheets went into the slip-sheet tray. No double-gripping, and no panels were dropped.

Alternating batches between mylar, poster boards, and butcher paper, the whole automation team watched and listened as the gripping team related their rise from discouragement to optimism over the past twenty four hours. Melissa was still carrying a straw around like a baton leading an orchestra.

Brandon's smile was for the success of the prototype,

and for the growth of the team including his newest hire.

For the next month, refinements were made, and work began on the other production units. The prototype was exercised continuously to check for endurance problems. One month before the production line was to be in full operation at LIC, the first machine was installed on the DES line and demonstrated. The customer was very pleased. Gad was in town for the demonstration. For four weeks prototype PCBs were fabricated on the new process lines and shipped to the phone assembly facility. Phones were tested and the green light was given for full production go-ahead.

The whole automation group from ICA was on hand for the jump to full PCB production at LIC. After a brief celebration, Brandon pulled-out some gifts; small boxes wrapped in butcher paper. He asked Melissa for her old cell phone then, with a smile, swapped it for a package.

Mentor Discussion and Exercises

Your experience as an engineer could be similar to Melissa's. You could be teamed with senior engineers to learn from them as well as to contribute new ideas from your perspective.

1. How did Aaron, Mike, and Melissa react, individually and as a whole, to surprises, setbacks

and problems?

2. Would you say that Aaron and Mike were good mentors?
3. Was Brandon a good manager?
4. How would you have led the team through each phase of this program?
5. What role did Mike play?
6. Should the most experienced person make all the decisions?

Product Development is an exciting adventure creating new or improved technologies, combining creative and academic skills, managing and nurturing relationships to bring the best out in everyone involved.

7. What engineering skills were necessary for this project?
8. What communication and personal skills were important?
9. Where did they go to get inspiration?
10. What did this team do well?
11. What could this team have done differently to be more successful?

Some engineering problems can be solved immediately, by applying good sense and skills; other problems take time, deep thought, experimentation, study, and conversation.

12. What happened when the team discovered that the

vacuum cup suction was reaching through the slip-sheet and gripping the adjacent panel?
13. What did the team do to solve the problem?

They experimented, adjusted variables, then took time to think, removing themselves from the present environment to rest and get fresh ideas.

14. Are all problems solved by one person, by the expert?
15. What is the advantage of working as a team?

If you like solving these types of problems and working with teams, you should seriously consider the satisfying profession of engineering.

2 - THE ORBITAL MECHANIC

"Dad, what a cool office." Kayla hopped into the high-back chair behind a handsome desk lined with little spacecraft models and rockets. "I didn't know you work in a place like this."

"Well," Dr. Thomas Dixon said to the fourteen-year-old, "I also spend some of my time in conference rooms and laboratories." Kayla's father carefully lifted a small model and glided it through the air in a curved path in front of his office window. The company marquee outside read, "Welcome to Bring your Child to Work Day."

"It seems extra bright outside." Dr. Dixon closed the blinds.

"I'm just glad to be out of school for a day." Kayla

said.

"Now," Tom thought, "how am I going to get her to see how exciting science is? He slid a chair right beside Kayla, tapped the space bar on his laptop keyboard, and typed a password.

"So dad, I know that you do something with spaceships, but whenever you leave papers around the house, all I see is circles and curves and numbers. Are you some kind of spacecraft artist?"

"I guess conic sections could be viewed as art,"[5] He thought, then turned to Kayla. "Not a traditional artist; I'd say I'm more of an architect, but I don't design buildings." Tom moved the mouse around, clicked a couple times, then pointed at the screen. "Look here. Do you recognize this?"

"Of course dad, it's our solar system."

"Right. Well, what do humans know about all these planets, and how did we get that information?"

"That's easy, we just search for it on the internet. I did a research paper last year on Pluto. Did you know it's not a planet any more?"

"So they say." Tom tightened his lips. "No one on Pluto told us what Pluto is like, and there's certainly no internet connection there, yet. What we know came from using telescopes and space probes to take pictures, and measure motion, and frequencies of light; then someone could put the information on the world-wide-

---

[5] Conic Sections are a set of mathematical relationships describing the parabola, ellipse, hyperbola, and circle.

web."

"Hey, do you think we'll ever have a solar-system-wide-web?"

"Likely!" Tom said with a smile, then patted his daughter on the back. "And maybe you'll be the one that invents it."

Kayla picked up one of the models on the desk. "So is that what these are, interplanetary space cameras?"

"Yes, but they do more than take pictures."

"So your company designs spaceships. What exactly do you do?"

"I decide what path or trajectory to take to get there."

"That doesn't sound too hard. Just launch it on a rocket, and point it at the planet you want to go to." Kayla turned when she heard her father laugh.

Tom clicked again and pointed. "Look here. This is called a interplanetary trajectory map. It's an overlay, kind of a road map printed on the solar system."

"One, two," Kayla pointed at the circles on the screen starting from the sun moving outward. "Three. This one is Earth, right?"

"Yes. Now as you know all these planets are moving around the sun. Our planet goes around the sun in..."

"I know dad, 365 days."

"That's my girl. The closer the planet is to the sun, the faster it orbits around the sun. If we want to go from Earth to, say Jupiter, we can't just aim for Jupiter, because it takes a number of months to get there, and Jupiter won't be there any more if we just point in that direction from the start."

Kayla squinted, then pointed at Earth's ellipse. "Why is the spaceship path from Earth to Jupiter going around the sun?"

"Kayla, what you're looking at is the very mission we are performing right now, in space. In fact, we are at an exciting time in our mission to Jupiter. The spacecraft is called *Vector1*." Tom pointed at Earth on the map. "We launched a year ago and in three days from now *Vector1* will pass by Earth on it's way out to Jupiter. It's been around the sun..."

"Wait. Why is *Vector1* coming back to Earth if it hasn't been to Jupiter yet?"

"It's called a gravity assist maneuver or fly-by. To get to great distances and speeds, we swing by planets and take some of their energy." Tom slowly moved his finger along the curve approaching Earth. "We fly in behind them and let the planets gravity accelerate the spacecraft and give it enough speed or energy to make it farther out into space, farther away from the sun. This way, we don't have to use as much rocket fuel; fuel is heavy and very expensive to lift into space."

Kayla wiggled in her seat and rubbed her nose. "So, you plan pathways that follow the planets, which speeds up the spacecraft to keep it going deeper into space."

"That's a simple view of it, but pretty much correct."

"But if you just come in behind the planet, why doesn't the planets gravity just pull it in and make it crash?"

"Very good question. We don't try to hit the planet

as we follow it. We point to the side a little so the planet does two things. It makes us go faster, and it turns or steers the spacecraft in the direction we want to go. The trick is approaching the planet just right."

"Kayla squinted her eyes a little and pinched her chin.

"Here, let me make it a little easier. Picture our big round trampoline at home. Now imagine it with a bowling ball resting right in the center. Now, suppose you and I are standing on opposite sides of the tramp. To roll a soccer ball from me to you, I would roll it along the trampoline so it passes just to the side of the bowling ball. What will the soccer ball do as it rolls along?"

"It will turn toward the bowling ball because that's downhill."

"Right. If it rolls too slow, it will turn too much toward the center, and hit the bowling ball. If it rolls fast or far away from the ball, it will pass by the bowling ball while turning toward it just a little. If I roll it even faster, it will turn a little and then roll off the far side of the tramp. Picture every planet as a bowling ball in the center of a trampoline causing things that come near to steer toward the planet. We can use these gravity pulls to turn and steer the ship where we want it to go."

"Cool." Kayla picked up a different model and held it high as she flew it around a globe in the corner of the room.

"And let's suppose the trampoline was orbiting around the house..."

Kayla raised her eyebrows. "Sorry dad, I can't imagine a trampoline orbiting our house."

Tom looked up for a moment. "Okay, try this. Remember when we all went skating? Suppose you and I were skating along and I was a little ahead of you. Now if I reached back and grabbed your hand, then pulled on you and swung you out in front of me, you would speed up and I would slow down a little, you would be going faster than you were before, and I would be going a little slower. That's what the planet does to the spacecraft."

Kayla closed her eyes half way. "It sounds like a lot of math."

"Yes, and physics and other important school subjects. But it's really powerful to know how to..."

"Dr. Dixon!" A man in his early twenties with a red face, out of breath, stood in the doorway of Tom's office.

"Hi Ben, how is your internship going?"

"I'll tell you about that later. We have a serious problem and I came to get you."

"What are you talking about?"

"There's been a solar flare, larger than expected. As programmed, *Vector1* computer systems automatically shut down for radiation protection."

Tom stood and moved quickly toward the window and parted the blinds.

Ben continued. "They're not sure if the solar panels retracted in time, the radio signal has gone quiet.

Anyway, the solar wind gave us a nudge, and they say she's approaching Earth high and wide."

"No!" Tom turned from the window, distinct wrinkles across his forehead. "This can't be. Everything was going well. We've worked so hard for this."

Ben opened the door wide. "The director wants the best orbital mechanic, in the control room, right now" Ben pointed at Tom and raised both eyebrows. "That means you."

Tom grabbed his laptop and headed for the door. "Kayla, come with me. It looks like 'Bring Your Child to Work Day' is not going to be routine." Tom pointed at the spacecraft Kayla was flying around the office. "Bring that model."

Kayla lowered the spacecraft and followed the two men quickly down a long hall.

"What happened Ben? We've experienced solar flares before. Why is she off course? Why do you think the solar panels are still extended?"

"That's the only explanation for the change in trajectory. And there's another problem; we don't know the spacecraft attitude..."

"A spacecraft with an attitude?" Kayla thought out loud, but the two men did not hear her. "Well if I had just been hit by solar wind, my attitude would be bad."

Tom and Ben entered the control room, with Kayla gravitating right behind. Her father pointed to a chair in the corner. "Ben, would you sit by my daughter? She'll probably have questions and I'll be too..."

"You got it Dr. TD." Ben replied.

"Dr. Dixon, the timing couldn't have been worse." A man with a dress shirt and loose tie sighed a small measure of relief when Tom entered the room. He pointed at a computer monitor. "From all we can tell, the solar wind had enough effect on *Vector1* to put our periapsis or perigee burn altitude too high."

"Kayla." Ben leaned over and spoke quietly. "Ask me anything you want."

"Why did you call my dad an orbital mechanic? That sounds like someone with wrenches on the space station that goes around fixing broken satellites."

Ben grinned. "An orbital mechanic uses math and physics to predict how planets, asteroids, and spacecraft react to the gravitational pull of each other."

"Oh. So that's how he can plan trips to Jupiter."

Tom leaned over and examined the screen. We're off by a few arc-seconds. [6] "We're on the wrong approach trajectory to Earth. We need a course correction burn immediately," Tom pronounced with a very serious tone, "or we'll be on the wrong departure trajectory leaving Earth; we'll be headed no-where at high speed."

"We can't maneuver within an hour," Another man, plaid shirt and blue jeans yelled from across the room. "*Vector1* is in radiation shutdown for fifty-five more minutes. And when she comes back on line, if she comes back on line, we don't even know her attitude, we

---

[6] An arc-second is an angular measurement equal to one-sixtieth of an arc-minute which in turn is equal to one-sixtieth of a degree.

could make things worse with a hasty burn. We could come in low and have aerodynamic drag in the Earth's atmosphere..."

Kayla looked at Ben.

Ben whispered. "A burn means to fire the on-board rockets to change it's direction or speed. It's often called a Delta-V or Delta-velocity."

"What are you talking about?" Dr. TD raised his voice.

"Tom, it's very possible that the solar panels were damaged by the flare. They weren't designed to take this much radiation. They were supposed to retract temporarily for events like this."

"I know all that. Are you telling me that our billion dollar mission is gonna fail because..."

"Okay, hold on everyone." The mission director demanded everyone's attention, then walked over to the whiteboard. He drew a small circle in the center surrounded by three slightly oval or elliptical circles, progressively larger representing the orbits of the planets out to Jupiter. He drew the flight path of *Vector1* starting from where the Earth was a year ago for launch, around the sun just past Venus, and approaching Earth's present position. He drew an X representing the position of *Vector1*, very close to Earth, then a dashed arc passing just outside Earth and on out to Jupiter.

"Why didn't he draw Mercury or Mars?" Kayla whispered.

"I'll tell ya' in a minute."

The director continued, "In three days, *Vector1* will make it's closest approach to Earth."

"That's called perigee" Ben said to Kayla.

"On it's current path her altitude will be too high." The director handed the marker to Tom. "What are our options? Let's get them all on the board."

"Wow, dads pretty important. He's got to figure out how to save this mission."

"Sometimes they call him Dr. TD for Touchdown when the probe hits the target. Or sometimes it's Dr. T for 'trajectory' because he's the best trajectory planner on the planet."

"Okay." Tom accepted the pen and moved to the board. "Is there anyway to command power-up any sooner than fifty-five minutes?"

Several head movements indicated no.

"Jerry, do we still have our full budget of extra fuel?"

"Yes, all prior burns have been planned, nominal, and within budget."

"If we could burn now, we could correct it with one burn, perhaps even in an hour." Tom drew a red curve from the X passing between Earth and the present trajectory.

"Remember Tom," a lady at one of the computers said, "once the computer powers up, it will take another thirty minutes for it to perform system checks and to confirm attitude. We can't burn until that's done."

"But you're not sure we have an attitude problem, right?" Tom asserted.

"That's true. If we knew the attitude was okay, we

could burn right after she wakes up."

"Can you give me a probability? What are the odds that *Vector1* is still at the right roll, pitch and yaw?

There was silence for ten seconds.

Ben held his hand out flat, palm down, in front of Kayla. "This is roll." Ben rotated his hand thumb down, then thumb up. "This is pitch." Ben pointed his finger tips downward, then upward. "This is yaw." He rotated his hand moving his finger tips left and right, keeping his palm pointed down.

Another man spoke up. "I'd say if both solar panels are still extended, then the solar wind would have acted equally about her CG"

"CG?" Kayla asked Ben.

"Center of Gravity. Kind of like the pivot point on a playground teeter-totter. If you push on both sides equally, then it won't rotate."

"Look." Tom used the blue pen and sketched another curve. "We can correct this problem using two Delta-V burns a couple hours from now, but we'll use most of our spare fuel. There won't be any margin for error later in the mission."

"That's not acceptable." The director patted a handkerchief on his forehead.

"We may be able to do it with one simple burn if we do it in one hour when *Vector1* wakes up. Is there any other way to ascertain her orientation?"

Again silence.

Kayla still held the model of *Vector1* in her lap, running her fingers over the solar panels. She turned to

Ben and whispered. "I remember a time when dad and I were out on the back patio of our house an hour after sunset looking for shooting stars. Dad pointed out a satellite passing slowly overhead reflecting sunlight from it's solar..." Kayla stopped and looked over toward her dad then mumbled. "Why don't they just look at it through a telescope."

Kayla grabbed Ben's arm. "Why don't they just look at *Vector1* through a telescope? Or a few telescopes?"

"I don't know. I haven't been here long enough to know if that will work. Usually space probes are too far away for a visual. But this one's close to Earth."

"Uh, Dr. Dixon." Ben raised his hand slowly. "Sir, I don't know if this is practical, but Kayla has a suggestion."

The director turned to Tom. "Who is this Tom?"

"This is my daughter, Kayla. She's here for..."

"This isn't a good time for a field trip." the director said.

"I know sir," Ben insisted, "but I think you may want to hear what she has to say."

"Okay young lady, if you're as smart as your dad, we need to hear it."

All eyes turned on Kayla.

"Well, my dad showed me a satellite one night flying overhead. The solar panels reflect the sun just after sunset if they're pointed in just the right way. If *Vector1* is close enough to the Earth, can't we look through telescopes and see how much the solar panels are reflecting?"

Several people in the room suddenly turned back to their computers and began typing.

"Ya, remember that time," someone in the room said, "that we needed to determine the condition of the Space Shuttle. We pointed lasers and telescopes from Patrick Air Force Base and they were able to see into the shuttle bay and..."

The room turned from silence to business. "Get on it people. Contact all the space surveillance sites and get those telescopes pointed at *Vector1*."

Dr. Tom looked over at his daughter and gave her a wink. The director nudged Tom's arm with his elbow.

Within fifteen minutes, the tracking stations began reporting.

"Affirmative!" The man in the plaid shirt called out. "Indeed, *Vector1* solar panels appear fully extended and her attitude unchanged by the solar flare."

Dr. TD began running simulations on his laptop to plan for the correct Delta-V needed right when *Vector1* came online.

Kayla and Ben were no longer sitting in the corner. Now an integral part of the team, they looked over shoulders at data on various controller screens. Optimistic tension still filled the room. Tom uploaded the burn parameters into the main flight computer.

"She's awake." yelled one of the controllers. "*Vector1* is back on line."

"Are you ready!" the Director said to Tom.

"We are 'go' for Delta-V burn." Tom replied.

"Proceed!"

Immediately, the command was issued. Within seconds, favorable telemetry signals were received. Within minutes it was confirmed; *Vector1* made the course correction successfully. The control room erupted with cheers. Kayla joined the high-five ceremony.

The good news, *Vector1* could continue on her journey to Jupiter; the bad news, there was a good chance her solar panels were damaged in the flare. This would reduce mission capability, but not crush it.

Ben elbowed the ninth-grader. "I think they should rename it, *Kayla-one.*"

Mentor Discussion and Exercises

1. Would you like to be the engineer, mathematician, or scientist that figures out how to get spaceships to distant worlds?

If so, you may want to consider a career in Orbital Mechanics, also known as Celestial Mechanics, or Astrodynamics. It's a great job. Engineers of this type must understand the laws of physics, mathematics, and computers. Dr. Dixon used all these tools to plan and simulate interplanetary trajectories. As a result, mankind gets more experience with space, and the truth about distant places.

2. What did you learn from this story?
3. Why does it take so long to get to Jupiter or other

planets?

4. Is there a way we can get there faster?
5. Why did Dr. Dixon send *Vector1* around the sun, past Venus, and back to Earth before going to Jupiter?
6. Why did the solar flare knock *Vector1* off course?
7. Could solar wind make that much difference?
8. Why was Kayla able to think of a solution when others didn't?

Everything we see and experience in our lives might help us solve a problem someday. Even in school, all of our classes give us knowledge and perspective to help us be more creative and aware. Next time you're in a math or science class, listen for terms like parabola, conic sections, or Newtons laws of motion. With tools like these, you could be The Orbital Mechanic that takes mankind to new and very distant places.

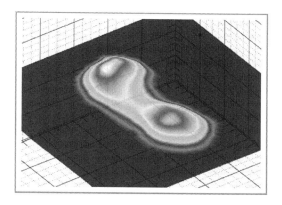

3 - FOOT NOTES

"Ken, why are you standing on the desk?" Joan said, laughing at her husband as she entered the home office finding him in a most unusual position. "And why is your foot on the printer?"

Ken's left foot was on his desk, right foot on the glass of the printer's built-in scanner, left hand gripping the back of the chair, and right index finger reaching for the scan button on the four-in-one device. The reclining office chair was wobbling back and forth.

"How em... embarrassing." He thought, trying to keep from falling. "I had a feeling she might walk in at the wrong time."

"Well, you've seen me do stranger things than this."

Ken shifted his weight. "It was part of the deal when you married an engineer."

Ken didn't look up, but imagined his wife smiling at his little joke. The scanner hummed as the light sensor moved slowly across the scanner under the glass supporting his foot. "If I could just hold steady for a few more seconds," he thought raising his chin slowly to look across the room.

Joan stood with eyebrows raised and hands on hips. "Well?" She repeated.

"We've got to find a better way of scanning the foot."

"Who does?"

"Scanner companies charge too much and won't tell us how to connect our computers to their scanners."

The chair began to roll away from the desk. Joan leaped forward and caught it keeping her husband from *breaking* his foot instead of scanning it.

"You're gonna need a different kind of scan if you're not careful."

Ken slowly lifted his foot from the scanner and placed it on the desk. Then he stepped onto the chair, then onto the floor never taking his eyes off the computer screen. He grabbed the mouse, kicked his shoe out of the way, sat in the chair, and leaned forward.

Joan, proud of her husband's engineering passion, stepped up behind him, kissed him on the top of his head, glanced at the screen and whispered, "I recognize that foot."

Figure - Desktop Scanner Bare Foot Image

He did not respond.

She leaned to one side so she could see his face. His eyes were fixed on the screen. She politely left the room.

Just five minutes earlier, Ken was sitting at his desk, sketching in his engineering log book, reviewing websites on commercial 3D scanners. "There has got to be a better way." He had thought. "We've tried other scanning methods available on the market and it's just not getting us anywhere. They are too expensive for our application and the manufacturers are too restrictive in how we use their scanners. There has got to be a way to capture the shape of the foot in a simple manner."

Ken had been thinking of various devices already on the market that capture images. "I wonder if I can use an existing device, something that is cheap, made in the millions and could accomplish the task." At that moment, he had leaned back in his chair and looked around the room. "What about a desk top scanner? There's one in almost every office, in every home for that matter." That's when, almost without thinking, he had pushed back his chair and stepped onto the desk.

Ken was working with an engineering team and entrepreneur on a project to make custom arch supports, or orthotics, in a matter of minutes, a process that at that time took weeks for the patient or customer to receive their custom insole. The full extent of the project was to create a quick way to scan the shape of the foot—the bottom of the foot to be more specific—make some prescriptive shape adjustments as prescribed by the foot doctor, then recreate the shape quickly in a plastic or composite orthotic or arch support. Ken was specifically working on the method to obtain the shape from the patient's foot. Other team members were working on the fabrication of the orthotic, a story for another time. (See Engineering Story: Quick Step)

"We've got 60 minute eye-wear, 30 minute photo finishing, why not 30 minute orthotics?" Ken rubbed his chin and stared at the image in front of him. "Is there some way to extract geometry from this image, exact skin distance from the scanner surface? The foot image is in focus anywhere the skin touches the glass, and progressively less focused along the sides of the foot where the skin doesn't touch the glass. Now there's something. Perhaps a software algorithm could be written to presume a z-value[7] or height as a function of the degree of focus. The greater the focus, the closer the skin is to the glass." He placed his left hand on the

---

[7] In this context, "z-value" refers to the distance of a point along the z-axis of an x, y, z coordinate system.

scanner and pressed the scan button. "I need another example."

After numerous attempts, Ken concluded that this method lacked precision.

"Suppose I illuminated the foot, different light intensities or colors at different elevations. The resulting scanned image would look like a topographical map, each color representing an elevation." This thought also had merit, but after 20 minutes and a few sketches, He turned the page and moved on.

Figure - Weather Stripping, Cloth and Foam Rubber

"What if I lay some kind of compliant or squishy sheet of material on the glass that has bumps or stripes, then as I push down with my foot, the bumps or stripes will squish and elongate different amounts depending on the foot pressure. Hey, that's worth trying."

Ken went into his garage and grabbed an old roll of weather stripping, the kind you put between the door and the door frame to prevent air flow into or out of the house. "Great, the weather stripping has self adhesive on the back. I'll cut a dozen pieces a little longer than the length of my foot and stick them side by side on a piece of cloth. Still, this is only going to capture parts of my foot that are within a half inch or so of the glass, the higher parts of my foot won't make an impression."

He noticed a piece of 1 inch thick foam rubber pad, still dirty from the last camping trip. "I'll add this between my foot and the weather stripping to diffuse the image and capture more depth."

Figure - Scanner Image of Foot Impression on Rows of Compressed Weather Stripping

Within thirty minutes, Ken was once again standing on his desk with his foot on the scanner, separated by weather stripping, cloth, and an inch of foam rubber. "Well, at least it feels nice." He carefully reached down and pressed the scan button.

The image was impressive, so he spent the rest of the

afternoon trying to figure out the mathematics of extracting z-values from the rows of black and white stripes which varied in width along the image.

While working on the math, other variations came to mind so he sketched them in the log, including the idea of a layer of round elastomeric beads, like a layer of rubber marbles, that would enlarge in diameter under pressure. He experimented with the idea of velcro hooks deflecting under pressure, and a couple of rubber door mats purchased at the home improvement store.

"None of these seem very practical." Ken wiped sweat from his forehead. "If we have to concede to an existing scanner company, how am I gonna face my team and our partner?" Even though the compressed weather stripping had possibilities, he was not enthusiastic. "We certainly can't have patients standing on home grade scanners. We would have to build one with thick strong glass. Can you imagine the conversation at the doctor's office? 'Thank you, I've scanned your insurance card, now would you please step up on the scanner so we can get your foot?' Besides, this isn't really the shape we want anyway. When a person is standing, their foot is compressed, the arch is partially collapsed. Our podiatrist[8] consultant said we need a way to capture the foot shape when only part of the patient's weight is on the foot, when the arch is still prominent."

Ken took a break for dinner but he didn't say much

---

[8] Foot physician.

to Joan. While eating peas she watched from the corner of her eye as he was carefully compressing one or two peas with his spoon. "What are the mechanical properties of peas?" he thought.

"What about a digital camera? Everyone has one. Can I take a picture of the bottom of my foot and extract the shape information somehow?" Reaching for his cell phone camera, he thought for a moment, then put it down. "What good will that do? It's about the same as a scanner, just quicker, with greater depth of focus."

Ken finally stopped playing with his food and ate it.

"I wonder how the other team is doing." He reflected for a few minutes on the rest of the project where the team was fabricating an orthotic on a pin mold. "I'll be right back." Ken said to Joan as he left the kitchen. He happened to have a piece of a pin mold prototype, one of the top or bottom guide plates with a large number of holes in it.

Returning to dinner, he examined the plate turning it over, rotating it to different angles. As he did so, occasionally light from the dining room chandelier would shine through, casting spots on the table. "What if I use this plate and a light source to cast an image of white spots on the bottom of the foot, take a picture and then use the spots to determine relative height all over the foot. This would be a relaxed foot image, but that's probably better than a weighted foot image."

"Joan, I need something round, like a ball, that I can shine spots on for an experiment."

"How about a cereal bowl, or a mixing bowl?"

"Yah, that would work. Let's try a small mixing bowl."

Ken had some past experience working with light and optics, so he found a lens from an old telescope, and a light source. He held the image plate near a bowl; (Joan allowed these kind of things if he promised to be careful). Then he shined the light through the guide plate. The white spots on the bowl were blurry because the light source was too large in diameter and too close to the plate. "I would need more of a *spot* light source to make crisp round images on the foot."

Ken tried flashlights with and without the reflector mirror, and small lights like LEDs, but they were not bright enough to get a good image with his camera.

Figure - White Spots on Bowl Cast by Light
Through Pin Mold Plate

"What about the sun?" He looked out the window.

"It's bright, located at essentially infinity, and almost a point source." Ken placed his camera on the guide plate, then the bowl upside down over the camera, and carried them out to the back patio to try the experiment. With the bowl on the table, the guide plate held in position with his left hand, and the camera in his right, he took several pictures of sun spots on the bowl, examining each one on the camera screen. This approach turned out to be the best by far, but after awhile, unable to determine how to produce a large number of crisp spots without the sun, he gave up on the spot image idea.

During the next team meeting, the memory of blurred spots on the bowl was still sharp in Ken's mind. He did not participate in the discussion but sat thinking. "The team's orthotic-forming device is essentially a 'bed of nails', a matrix of steel pins held in place by friction between two guide plates. For forming, each pin is pushed into place by a machine, creating the overall foot shape."

He grabbed a complete pin mold and pushed pins back and forth, repeatedly with his fingers.

"What if I reverse the process." he thought. "And use a foot, an actual foot to push the pins, then somehow measure the position of each pin and capture this information in the computer?"

Ken took his shoe off, crossed his right leg over his left, and pressed the pin mold against the bottom of his right foot. Either his behavior or the smell drew the attention of his team mates, but they went on with their meeting. With some wiggling, feeling the pins work their way between his toes, the pins slowly moved. Before long, the pin mold reflected the shape of his foot. "Nice massage," he thought.

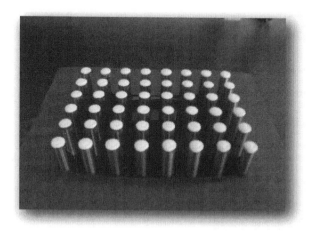

Figure - Small Matrix of Dowel Pins with White Painted Tips

"Now, how am I going to measure the position of each pin, quickly?"

He asked one of his team mates if there was a pin mold he could borrow for experimentation and received a small prototype. It only had 48 pins, but it would allow him to think through some possibilities.

Back at his home office, Ken played with the little mold, by pressing various objects against the pins and considering how the shape could be digitally extracted.

"If I take a photograph from the side," he thought. "I will only be able to see the first row, and perhaps a few other pins that are extending higher than the first row. So that won't work. If I take a photograph from directly above, I really won't be able to see how high each pin is standing."

He rotated the pin mold with his fingers to various angles.

"Suppose I take a picture of the mold at an angle between a front view and a top view, such that I can see the tip of every pin? Can I use this image to get the z-values?"

He sketched the small pin mold and placed coordinate axes x, y, and z on the illustration. He recalled from a math class something named the parametric line formula. "I think it was linear algebra." Ken went to a shelf in his closet where he kept a few old textbooks, but it wasn't there, so he searched online for the basic description of the parametric line formula. "These online math sites are great. I didn't have to memorize everything I learned in school. I just need to know the terminology so I can find it on a trustworthy site."

He also remembered from a class in image processing software that, whether viewing a straight line directly off to the side (orthogonally), or at some arbitrary angle, it still appears to the viewer as a straight line! "If I use the fact that each pin has a known, unchanging X and Y value, and that the only thing changing in the image is the Z value, and it only takes two points in space to define a line, I can use the spot, the end of each pin, to determine where each pin is located along it's pre-defined line in space."

He grabbed his digital camera and took several images of the pin mold from different angles. Unfortunately the pin tips didn't show up very well in the pictures. Undaunted, Ken went on searching and solving one problem after another.

"What can I do to increase the contrast between the dowel pin tips, and the rest of the image?"

He went into the garage and surveyed cans of house paint with hardened drippings down the sides, grabbed the closest screw driver, opened a can and poured a small puddle of pale yellowish-white paint on a piece of plywood and then carefully dipped the tips of all 48 pins. "Now the ends will show up much brighter than the sides... I hope."

Staring at the painted tips didn't make them dry faster, but the image of rows and columns of perfectly aligned white dots was etched into his mind. After the paint dried, he took a few more digital images and was satisfied with the paint job.

Back at his desk, thinking through the process, he realized the solution. "All I need is two reference points P1 and P2, two known Z values for each pin. I can get that by taking two reference pictures, one when all the pins are retracted or lowered, and another when all the pins are fully extended or at their highest position, making sure the pin mold and the camera stay in the same place for all the pictures. Using these two digital images, the line in space of each pin will be known. Then, I can shape the mold like a foot, take a third picture, measure the relative distance t, from one of the reference pins, multiply by the total distance between the reference pins, and there is the Z value for that pin. Cool!"

Ken used a tennis ball to test his theory. He created a way to hold the pin mold body steady and fixed relative to the camera for all three images. That was the easy part. The hard part was processing the bitmap image file, extracting the white pixels from among the black.

He had written software before, but felt challenged. To make it as foolproof as possible, adjustments were made to image brightness, contrast, and other parameters.

Figure - Inverted Images of Small Pin Mold at Retracted, Spherical, and Extended Pin Positions

To test his method, Ken plotted the image of the pins , then mathematically analyzed the image to obtain the ball diameter. "It worked. The virtual ball is the same diameter as the actual tennis ball."

Excited, he then generalized the approach for a larger mold, a device as large as his foot.

"The lower the camera angle, the more accurate the z-value will be." He surmised. "But if the camera angle gets too small, then I won't be able to see over the horizon (or under the horizon if you prefer) and get the details on the far side of the foot."

This didn't puzzle him too long. "What about two images of the same foot, one from each side?" Two cameras would capture the image as fast as one camera, he thought. "Wait, what about mirrors to split one image and capture both angles with one picture?"

Ideas came fast—too fast to remember them all. Ken sketched everything he thought (except for the peas at dinner), knowing finally he was on a solid path to victory. Like rolling the perfect ball at the bowling alley, halfway down the lane you just know it will be a strike. As one drawing evolved into another, he converged on the final solution: an inexpensive webcam (camera) that faced down toward two angled mirrors that split the image back upward toward two vertical mirrors. The two vertical mirrors were drawn mounted parallel to the walls of a box all about twice the size of a shoe box. The pin mold was mounted in the top of the box with the white painted pin tips pointing down. "As the patient steps on the pins, a negative impression will be made on the top of the pins with an almost exact replica of the foot on the white painted tips on the bottom."

He got on the phone immediately and described the box to another team member. Within two days, the prototype box was built and ready for mirror, lights, and camera installation. While waiting, he had to figure out how to illuminate the white pins inside the dark box so that the only thing on the picture would be white spots with no stray light. He tried a string of Christmas lights —the little ones the size of birthday candles. Then he took his traditional tour of the hardware store looking for ideas and found decorative light strips that would do the job.

He also obtained a full size pin mold from the team and carefully dipped the entire set of pins in a thin puddle of paint to create hundreds of white tips. It was a challenge to mount everything in the box, keeping mirror angles just right, camera firmly fixed, and lights mounted to optimize pin tip illumination while minimizing optical noise. The first images were less than perfect, but demonstrated promise.

"How can I get rid of all these random spots cluttering the picture?" he thought.

Ken removed all the components from the box and spray painted the entire inside flat black, as well as any other items he didn't want to show up in the picture. By the next day, "Wow! Great images."

He then began work on the software algorithm to extract the z-value of each pin, thinking again through the process in great detail. "The first step is to find the first pin of the first row. Then I'll move inward toward the center of the foot to find the next spot in the row and just keep repeating this process until I reach the center of the foot. I can extract the data for the whole foot if I do this for each row and each side of the foot."

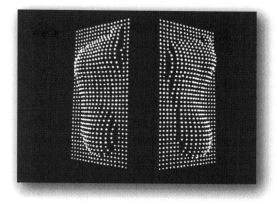

Figure - Pin Mold Scanning Box Images Showing
Foot Shaped Pin State

After defining a basic algorithm, Ken and the team
met with a software expert to complete the task. Shortly
thereafter, the team was producing frequent graphic
images of foot impressions made on the pin mold
scanner.

More prototypes were made, and after weeks of
iterations on the concept, the team had a stable,
repeatable process for capturing foot shapes (their own
feet) from impressions in the pin mold. Even the
entrepreneurs stepped in for a scan. The final solution
had the added benefit that the pin mold used for
receiving impressions of a patients foot was nearly
identical to the mold used to fabricate orthotics (less the
paint). All components, except the custom black painted
box, were commercial off-the-shelf items totaling less
than a couple hundred dollars. The goal of creating a

foot scanner that was inexpensive and easy to interface with the rest of the orthotic machine was achieved.

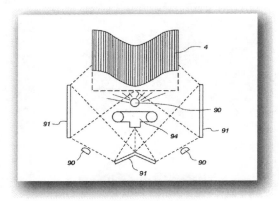

Figure - Patent Application Illustration of Pin Mold Imaging System [Ref: Patent US20090273109]

One night, under much less pressure, Ken was back at his home office feeling creative again with the original prototype. "I wonder what would happen if I use this thing on my face?" he thought.

"Hey Joan, look!"

"Wow, can I give it a try?"

Joan put her head in about the place where the pin mold would go while Ken clicked the capture button on the webcam software.

"Let me guess." Joan said. "You're now thinking of using this thing to make statues."

Mentor Discussion and Exercises

The dialog, conversation and thoughts in this story are fictionalized, but the results are real, and the inventive progression is very typical of most design projects experienced by the author. In most cases the project starts with a need or problem, in this case the absence of an economical and easy to interface foot scanner. The team did the right thing looking for existing scanner solutions that could be used to capture foot geometry or shape data.

1. What was wrong with the existing foot scanners on the market? Why wouldn't one of them work?
2. Faced with the need to develop a scanner from scratch, how did Ken start? What criteria did he use?

He looked at existing, low cost methods for image capture and began considering ways to obtain shape data from them.

3. What would you have done differently? Can you think of several ways to obtain foot shape data that Ken did not think of?
4. What did Ken use to expand his options? Where was he, and what was he doing when new ideas came?
5. How did every day objects play a role? Where would you go to see how things are done?

We call this benchmarking.[9]

6. What role did others play in Ken's work? Who did he interact with? Did this help or hinder the creative process?
7. What skills did Ken need or use in this project?
8. He had the ability to sketch his ideas; was this helpful?
9. He used mathematical models. In what way was this useful?

Engineering is a great adventure where we are faced with real world challenges and the opportunity and skill to find solutions. There is great satisfaction in climbing these mountains of opportunity, struggling, learning, achieving and making the world a better place. The challenges are endless, and the satisfaction is great.

---

[9] "Benchmarking is the study of existing products with functionality similar to that of the product under development... " Ulrich and Eppinger, *Product Design and Development,* McGraw-Hill, 4th Edition.

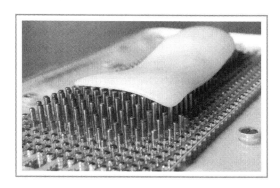

4 - QUICK STEP

"I hardly slept last night," Glenn said, placing the pin mold onto the vacuum press. "I have lived and relived this day for weeks."

Craig lifted the press door up while Glenn carefully aligned the new device.

"I'll tell you what," Craig said, "the day we first met with the customer, I saw how something like this could really help people." Craig glided his fingers lightly across the rounded tips of the polished pins, collectively resembling the bottom of a foot.

It was 6:30 am. The winter darkness still blackened the only window in the lab.

Glenn and Craig, two mechanical engineers, arrived before the rest of the team to get a head start testing the new forming device, a precision assembly of six-hundred and sixty-six stainless steel dowel pins,[10] completed just the night before.

"This is going to change the game for foot doctors and their patients." Glenn aligned a thin rubber sheet over the pin mold in the press then paused and looked up at the simple cooking oven sitting on the work bench. "I didn't think we were going to get the pin mold to work."

Craig looked up at his team mate, both eyebrows raised. "The hardest part was getting the top and bottom plates drilled accurate enough for the pins to slide freely up and down through both plates."

Glenn lifted a half filled bucket of water and placed it on the workbench next to the press. "I know. Bill went through four sets of plates trying to get it right."

"My biggest worry was the friction strips between the plates." Craig said. "We tried everything we could think of, different materials, different sizes, to get the pins to stay put after being shaped like a foot. But I feel good about this solution. We're set for the big demonstration in three weeks."

I hope you're right, Glenn thought, checking the timer and placing his finger tips near the oven door without touching. "Who was it that thought of using strips of rubber material between the pins?"

"I think it just came out in one of our brainstorm sessions. As I remember, when our first attempt didn't

---

[10] Long slender cylindrical rods.

work, we considered all kinds of things from the hardware store that we could put between the pins to get the right amount of friction..."

The bell on the oven rang.

Craig looked up at the tilted clock hanging from the corrugated steel wall of the old engineering lab. "Was that five minutes?"

Figure - Clear Hot Plastic Sheet over Smoothing Layer on Pins. Photo by Jaren Wilkey, Used by Permission

"Actually, I went thirty seconds longer this time to make sure the temperature was uniform all the way through the plastic." Glenn grabbed the chrome handle on the clear oven door and looked down at the workbench. "Where are the gloves? Never mind." Glenn reached in the oven, quickly removed a drooping transparent sheet of plastic, placed it on the rubber layer already on the pins then plunged his hands in the bucket of water.

"Ouch!"

While still holding the door up, Craig flipped a switch on the vacuum press. A low frequency rumble confirmed the pump was running. "Ready?"

Glenn moved back and Craig lowered the lid allowing its rubber sheet or bladder to lay across the plastic on the pin mold. He pressed the frame down against the vacuum table. As air evacuated from the mold area, the rubber bladder in the lid compressed against everything beneath it. Within seconds, they saw the unmistakable shape of the pin mold through the rubber, and then the shape of the foot...

"Somethings wrong."

"Uh-oh," they called out in unison.

"The shape is collapsing, the pins are slipping," Craig said. "There's too much vacuum! Shall I turn it off?"

"Yes, but it's too late. The shape is already gone." I was afraid that would happen," Glenn thought. "We'll have to try another one. Let this one cool and harden, then we'll make some notes and decide what to do." Glenn reached into the bucket, grabbed a wet rag, rung it out, then placed it on the hot rubber bladder under which the orthotic[11] (for a very flat-footed person) was cooling. A drop of sweat formed on his forehead. He then sat on a stool, eye-brows slightly lowered, chin on

---

[11] A brace or support for a limb of the body.

his fist, and eyes fixed on the vacuum press. "I wonder if anyone calculated the amount of force pushing down on the pins, and compared it with the total pin friction?"

Craig made some notes in the test log.

For the next hour, Glenn and Craig repeatedly reshaped the pin mold, tweaked the vacuum level, adjusted the oven temperature, varied the heating time, and created six more orthotics. Each one failed.

"We're doomed." Craig stood by the work bench, hunched over like someone kicked him in the stomach six times with six flattened orthotics. "I thought for sure this would work. What are we gonna tell Bill and Jake? What are we gonna tell our customer?"

When Jake and Bill arrived, the lab was a little warm for 8 a.m.

"Good morning guys," Jake said, sniffing the air. "Hey, you look like you've been up all night."

Bill looked down at the six pieces of white warped plastic on the work bench. "What is this? Are these old test samples, or have you been using the new mold?"

"Craig and I came in early, and..." Glenn looked carefully at Craig, "We have a problem."

Bill raised his head sharply. "You didn't break the mold did you?"

The four team members hovered around the work bench.

Craig pointed at the data in the test log. "We tried everything, different vacuum levels, different temperatures. Every time, the pins slipped."

"The friction in the pin mold seems to be pretty consistent for all the pins," Glenn added. "But it's not strong enough to hold, even against the lowest practical vacuum."

"I wonder," Bill lifted the pin mold to eye level and closed one eye. "I wonder if the vacuum is having some kind of effect on the rubber friction material, you know, causing it to slip when the vacuum is on?"

"Hadn't thought of that," Glenn said.

"Do you think the strips of rubber need to be thicker," Craig offered in desperation, "you know, larger diameter?"

"Or harder," Bill said.

"Okay," Jake interrupted. "These are all good questions, let's make sure we think through each one and not miss any important ideas." Jake took a deep breath. "Since there's no reason to jump right back into testing without some idea of how we're gonna fix this, let's take our lab books into the conference room and go through this a step at a time. Bill, will you bring the pin mold? Glenn, do you have a convenient copy of the requirements, the specification?"

Glenn nodded, looking in the back cover of his lab book for a loose piece of paper. "Yeh, I've got it." He then thought, "I don't know if I updated it after the last design review. It should be okay."

Other people were now coming into the lab, so Jake shut the door after all four were in the conference room, tossed last nights pizza boxes on top of the waste basket, and walked over to the whiteboard.

"All right," Jake began. "We've got three weeks until our customer demonstration. Other parts of the project are going well, right Bill?"

Bill nodded, gently putting the pin mold on the table.

Jake continued. "Suggestions on how we should proceed? I'm thinking we should review how we got to this point."

"Good idea," Glenn said. "I think we need to calculate the amount of force pushing down on the pins by the rubber bladder."

"Good. But first, would you please read the original requirements for the pin mold. Let's see if we overlooked something."

"Okay," Glenn pulled the wrinkled paper from his book, grabbed the two short ends, and dragged it back and forth across the edge of the table, then adjusted his glasses. "Okay, there are 27 requirements--"

Jake stopped him. "Just the ones that have something to do with shape, pressure, or vacuum. Use your best judgment."

Glenn read the list out loud.

"1, Allowable vacuum on the mold, maximum 70,000 Pascals. 2, Allowable heat on the mold, maximum 300 degrees Fahrenheit. 3, User friendly... No not that one."

Glenn skimmed down through the list.

"8, Allowable time for cooling, 120 seconds. 20, minimum pin travel, 1 inch. 26, accuracy of pin positioning, 0.063 inches. 27, material thickness ranges--"

Glenn looked up. "There really isn't a requirement that specifies how much pin friction there should be."

Bill said, "That's because requirements aren't supposed to assume how the mold is designed. If the specification said something about pin friction, then that would exclude designs that don't use pins."

"I already knew that." Glenn said.

"So why don't we just increase the friction," Craig said, "so the pins won't move under vacuum. That will guarantee that the shape will hold at other times."

"Look," Bill grabbed the pin mold and began pushing pins back and forth. "If you increase the friction too much, then the machine that pushes all the pins into position will need to be more powerful, bigger actuators, it will run our costs up, and it will probably take longer to form each foot shape. What is the requirement for forming time?"

"Let's see," Glenn looked down the list. "Here it is," 22, Allowable time to generate surface, maximum 180 seconds."

Everyone looked at Bill. "How long does it take now?"

"I don't know exactly," Bill said. "We haven't tested that part yet but initial estimates are about two minutes at best."

"Okay," Jake said. "Let's review the ideas we had that led up to using rubber strips between the pins, and let's look for ways to make the friction force lighter during pin positioning, and stronger during vacuum forming. Look through your lab books and let's list them. Craig will you writes these on the board?"

The team worked for an hour recalling the various concepts associated with retaining pin position and mold shape. As the whiteboard filled with color, the room filled with pen odor. There were times of progress, and times of frustration as the hour passed.

Ideas came slower, fewer and far between. Normally that would be good if everyone was writing or sketching and getting lots of good ideas down in their lab books, but voices as well as pens and pencils turned quiet. Eyes were glassing over with discouragement.

"I have a suggestion." Glenn removed his glasses and rubbed his eyes. "I suggest we break, go on our own and look for ideas. I think I'd like to go to the hardware store and just walk up and down the isles looking for things that lock or clamp or have friction."

"I agree," Jake said noticing nods from each team member. "Let's go to where ever our creative places are. I think I'll go to the sporting goods store. I need to pick up a tube for my bike anyway."

"I like to browse through auto parts," Craig said, "but I'm gonna stop by my home first."

"How about you Bill?"

"Well, I'm gonna get online and search through some supplier catalogs."

"I know we'll find a solution. Let's meet back here tomorrow morning, 8:00 a.m." Jake rallied the team as they left the conference room. "Look for things, anything that has a part that moves in a straight line, in some kind of linear motion, and stops or locks at an infinite number of positions. There's gotta be things like that at home, in the garage, in a car, in tools, look everywhere. Craig, when you're at home, see how window blinds can be set at any desired opening height. Alright?"

Glenn held back near the vacuum press after the others left, putting things away, sketching in his book, reviewing the list on the board, flipping through the test log. He even sorted through odds and ends in the storage cabinet looking for ideas. He caught himself clicking his ball-point pen in and out, then thought, "I wonder what mechanism latches the pen at the two positions, retracted and extended? Wait, my mechanical pencil can hold the led at any position." He pulled the pencil from his shirt pocket and examined the led motion repeatedly clicking the other end. He disassembled it, made some notes, put it back together, then headed for the door.

"Our customer will be really disappointed if we can't get this to work." Glenn thought, driving a little slower than usual to the hardware store. He reflected on the image of a young man the team met three months ago with Cerebral Palsy. In his mind Glenn saw the boy's involuntary but happy facial gestures, feet and hands mildly deformed, slight slouch while sitting, anxious about the attention he received for special shoes and orthotics, a gleam in his eyes. "Such a happy boy. He'll be heart broken."

Glenn remembered how the orthotic machine was intended to create special arch supports for any person in need of a custom flexible insole, but the machine was especially intended to help the boy with CP.

"Can I help you find something?" An assistant at the hardware store interrupted Glenn's seemingly mindless wandering.

"Oh, no thank you." Glenn replied then thought, "I know what my wife would say; why is it men never ask for directions."

He turned around quickly. "Sir, actually I'm working on a science project. I'm looking for things that have some kind of clamping device as part of the way they work. Can you think of anything like that in the store?"

The assistant did not look surprised at the question. "Perhaps he's heard that line before," Glenn thought.

"Well," making gestures with his hands. "Over in the tool section, Isle 7 and 8, you can find bar clamps, wood-screw clamps, and things like that. And over in plumbing, uh, Isle 22, they have hose clamps, you know those band type strips of metal that wrap around hoses to clamp them to pipes, like the radiator hose in your car."

"Thanks, I'll start with plumbing and then go to tools."

Glenn walked a little faster. "Hose clamps look pretty useful, but I can't see wrapping a tiny clamp around each pin and then adjusting all of them to change the friction."

On the way from Isle 22 to Isle 8, Glenn passed by the garden section and noticed rakes and shovels hanging handle-up side-by-side from a bracket. "Now there's something," Glenn thought. "I saw one of these in Craig's garage. You insert the handle upward from below and you can push it as high as you want, let go and it will stay in place." Glenn pushed up, then pulled down on a rake handle. "It looks like there's some kind of,... oh I see, there's a wedge shape, a piece of rubber that pivots away from the handle when pushing up, then it binds or pushes into the handle on the way down. I wonder if this could be done on miniature pins?" Glenn made a quick sketch in his lab book. (Yes, he brought his lab book to the hardware store.)

In the tool section Glenn walked very slowly looking up and down each rack of all kinds of tools. Noticing a familiar instrument, he thought, "Carpenters measuring tape." He picked up a basic model, pulled the tape from the body then let it retract. "Look at the thumb latch. You pull the tape out, push on the latch and it binds the tape against the inside surface, so tight I can't even push the tape back in without it buckling." Another entry was make in his book.

"Hey, what is that?" Glenn forgot he was in public. "Contour gauge? I've heard of these, a long set of little parallel pins that are right next to each other, like a hundred tiny soldiers standing in a row. It's used to measure the shape of wood moldings. I think my dad has one of these he uses to check the shape of wood turnings, like table legs or stair posts." Being careful not to wrinkle the wrapping, Glenn turned a small thumb screw on the side of the contour gauge. "Looks like the sides clamp on the pins to keep them in place. Wow, something like this might work. I wonder if we could stack a whole bunch of these side by side creating a clamp-able pin matrix." Glenn pulled out his cell phone and took a picture of the contour gauge then put it back on the shelf.

Finally at the wood clamp display, Glenn thoughtfully examined the various types including bar clamps, wood-screw, and spring clamps of all sizes. "I can't imagine how anything like these could be made small enough for what we need." Feeling discouraged, Glenn turned from the clamps to look at other tools. Just down by his feet on the bottom shelf he saw a familiar device. "Hey, that's what we used last week to seal around our leaking vent pipe." Glenn picked up a caulking gun and examined the linear ratcheting mechanism and realized that it could be set in just about any position and hold the force of the caulking or sealant tube pushing back on the plunger. Again, having doubts about using such a scheme on tiny pins caused him to return the tool to the shelf.

"The best concept I've found is the contour gauge. "Turning about, Glenn grabbed the cheapest one on the shelf and headed for checkout. He bought the gauge and a soda as a reward for his efforts then headed back to the office to refine his sketches.

"Donuts! Who brought donuts?" Craig said as he came into the conference room.

"Good morning everyone." Jake opened the box and pushed it towards Craig. The smell of a dozen variety donuts filled the room. "I thought this would help the creative juices this morning. Speaking of juices..." Jake gave each person a juice pouch."

"Thanks Jake." Each said in turn.

"Okay, no rules this morning. We'll just go 'round the room, take turns, and name one thing we learned or discovered yesterday, and then we'll go around again until everyone has listed everything they came with." Jake held up a whiteboard pen and said, "Craig?"

Craig, looking slightly disappointed chomping on a donut, got up and came to the board.

"I don't care how you organize them, just list every idea that is said. Here, I'll go first. At the sporting goods store I looked at rope climbing equipment and saw a device that only allows the rope or cable to go through it in one direction and locks on the rope in the other direction. It's called a vertical shuttle. Rock climbers use them as a safety device, I think."

Craig wrote on the board.

"Okay Glenn, you next"

"Your idea reminded me of one I saw at the hardware store, and I've also seen it in Craig's garage."

Craig turned around.

"It's a horizontal bracket that you mount on the wall to hang tools like rakes and shovels--"

"Oh yah," Craig mumbled. "That is so handy, my tools used to be piled in a corner in a big mess, falling down all the time."

"Craig, just write the idea on the board."

"Okay, Bill?"

"Well, I spent some time on the internet looking at hardware, tools, and industrial stuff. One thing led to another and I found myself at a hobby shop website looking at the pin art toy, remember, the one you can press against things and it will take an imprint of your face or your hand. Anyway, I searched the internet for 'pin art' and found one that comes with a locking motor."

"A motor?" Craig asked.

"Yah, I don't know how it works but apparently after you shape the pins, you flip a switch and something inside clamps all the pins."

"Really?" Jake said with an ascending high pitch. "How could we get ahold of one? How much was it?"

"I don't know, the price wasn't listed but I could try to find out."

"Please do and let's see if we could get one."

With a drink in one hand, Craig wrote 'Motorized Pin Art' on the board with the other.

"Craig, its your turn."

"I asked the guy at the auto parts store if he could think of any parts that clamp on other parts."

"That's exactly what I asked the guy at the hardware

store." Glenn didn't speak.

Gesturing with his hands Craig continued, "He walked down the isles with me and we looked at battery terminal clamps, radiator hose clamps, wire ties, bungie cords,--"

"Craig," Jake interrupted. "Please write all those on the board."

"There were a few tools like vice-grips that I looked at, but, I don't know, I didn't see anything that really jumped out as a possibility."

"Okay it's my turn again," Jake said. "In the bike section, I fiddled with bicycle brakes for a while wondering if the brake pads that clamp on the tire rim could be somehow developed into a series of little brakes to hold our pins. To be honest, I couldn't see--" Jake stopped himself. "Oh, we shouldn't pass judgment when we are brainstorming."

"Glenn?"

Glenn pulled out the contour gauge and put in on the table next to the pin mold. The other three leaned toward it. Bill took his donut out of his mouth and everyone sat their drinks on the table.

"I've seen one of those before," Craig said looking at Glenn. "Over at your dads house--"

"Yah, I know. My dads a carpenter and they use this kind of a device to capture the shape of wood moldings, using it as a template to duplicate the shape in another piece of wood." Glenn knelt down on the floor by the wall and pressed the stack of pins against the base molding along the wall. He carefully twisted the thumb screw then came back to the table. "See, the pin tips collectively follow the profile of the moulding and the clamping mechanism holds them in place." Glenn passed the device around. "Please don't get donut glaze on it. I was thinking that perhaps a whole set of these could be mounted side by side to make a two-dimensional matrix, and then we could somehow loosen all the clamps, drive all the pins to the shape we want, then lock them all to retain the shape during vacuum."

"Wow, okay, let's get that on the board and we'll come back and discuss it in detail."

"Bill, what else do you have?"

"Well, it's kind'a like the bike brakes. Going up the elevator yesterday, I was recalling how elevators are essentially a big linear device and they have an emergency brake system on each elevator car. It's a caliper or pinching type brake, like disc brakes on an automobile that slides along a vertical rail. If the primary cable drive system fails, the clamps engage on the vertical rail preventing the elevator from falling."

"I get it." Craig wrote the idea on the board.

The meeting continued as the donuts disappeared. None of the ideas or discussion yet produced an optimism that got the whole team excited. To the contrary, the team seemed as discouraged as they were the day before.

"I have one more," Craig said. "Well, I've mentioned it before but I think its worth listing again. While playing with bungie cords I was reminded of the cord stretching idea where we stretch the rubber cord between the pins to change the amount it presses on each pin. So I picked up a variety of rubber bands and tubes of different sizes, even surgical tubing, and experimented with the idea in our old prototype. It kind of works, but its got some problems. Anyway, I took a picture of it."

The team gathered around Craig as he pointed to and described the various features.

"It looks like a nice idea," Glenn said. "What problems did you see?"

"When you pull or stretch a band, since the band is pinched between all the pins in that row, it starts to stretch first at the outer pins towards the end, and the last pins to be released are towards the center of the row so the clamping and releasing is not uniform. I don't know if that's a problem, but it's something I noticed."

After a few moments of discussion, rubber band pulling, then silence, most eyes wandered back to the whiteboard.

"Let's get out of this room for a few minutes and stand around the press." Bill suggested and no one objected.

"Glenn and Craig," Jake said, "let's go ahead and repeat what you did yesterday morning."

Craig objected and Jake refined his suggestion.

"Well, at least stack up the pieces and let's have a look."

"Okay," Glenn said. We put the plastic orthotic in

the oven to heat at 250 degrees Fahrenheit for five minutes or so. We shaped the pin-mold like this." Glenn pressed the bottom of the mold against a plaster foot cast to force the pins into a foot shape on the top side of the mold. "We put on the smoothing layer, then put the hot plastic orthotic on top of that, then closed the rubber bladder."

To demonstrate, Craig lowered and clamped the door but did not turn on the vacuum.

Glenn sucked the rest of his drink collapsing his juice pouch.

"So when you evacuate it, the rubber is pulled down against the pins pushing all of them down." Jake talked to himself out loud.

Glenn was still sucking on his empty drink when Bill pointed right at Glenn's face and cried, "That's it! Look at Glenn's drink. We need to put the mold in a bag."

"What?" Everyone looked at Bill with contempt then at Glenn. "What are you talking about?"

"Glenn, suck harder on that straw!"

Glenn puckered and pulled as much air out of the drink bag as he could.

Figure - Evacuated Drink Bag showing Pressure on Both Sides of Straw

"Look," Bill continued. "Look at the shape of the bag surrounding the straw. The bag is pushing equally on both sides of the straw. If we put the pin mold inside a flexible vacuum bag, then the force on the pin tips on the top will be balanced by the force on the pin tips on the bottom. It's perfect."

"I get it." Craig said. "Keep doing that Glenn. "We've been putting the mold on a hard surface in the vacuum press. We need to put the mold on a flexible surface and let the vacuum pull up on that surface while it is pulling down on the top bladder. Wow, thats great."

Jake listened intently and the feeling in the lab changed in a few seconds from near hopelessness to cautious optimism.

"How did we overlook that?" Glenn said, after playing with the concept a few more times, finally taking the straw out of his mouth. "Bill, you are amazing. Look, we don't necessarily have to put the mold in a bag, we just need to make a box that the mold fits into with rubber bladders on both the top and the bottom."

"I see." Bill said.

Glenn opened his lab book and began to sketch with everyone hovering. His enthusiasm caused him to draw faster than usual so the result was not as clean as is typical for Glenn, but there was no holding back. He drew the top and bottom plate, the pins, a box in which the mold could rest, then a removable frame and bladder on the top, and a fixed frame and bladder on the bottom.

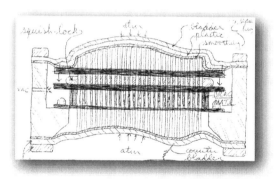

Figure - Engineering Sketch of Pin Mold Box with Top and Bottom Rubber Bladders. BYU Capstone Logbook, Used by Permission

"That is so cool." Jake said. "Bill, thanks for

watching how Glenn drinks. Glenn, thanks for playing with your food. Bill, how soon do you think you could build a box like this?"

Bill stopped and responded to his emotions. "I can't believe it, we don't even have to change the pin mold design for this; this is awesome. All this time, we've been focused on pin friction and clamping pins. This solution is so elegant."

"Glenn," Bill continued. "If you could do a detailed sketch of the box, I can get it built in a day or two. We're gonna need a vacuum pump."

"Can't you use the one on this press?" Jake asked.

"It would be better to buy a pump so we can run the plumbing directly to the box and hook it up exactly where we want it. When I was online yesterday, I saw some vacuum pumps at..."

"Hey, let me take care of that," Craig offered. "I know the required vacuum level. I'll go down to the local store and pick it up along with the tubing and fittings that we'll need."

"Thanks Craig," Jake summarized. "Okay, Glenn will do the drawing, Bill will make the new molding box, Craig will get the pump, and I will get some more plastic material for orthotics. When can we have it all ready for testing?"

Three days later, 7:30 p.m., the team had the final bladder mounted to the new box, and all the vacuum plumbing ready to go.

"Let's do it." Craig cheered.

Figure - Heating Oven, Upper Bladder in white, Lower Bladder in blue. BYU Capstone Files, Used by Permission

Craig held the vacuum top bladder while Glenn carefully aligned the pin mold in the box. Jake and Bill looked on anxiously.

"I'll tell you what, from the day we first met with the customer, I could see how this could really help people." Craig lightly glided his finger tips across the pins shaped like a foot.

Glenn placed the smoothing sheet over the pins then reached under the box and felt with the tip of his fingers, the new rubber bladder on the bottom of the box.

The oven bell rang.

Ready with gloves, Glenn retrieved the hot plastic from the oven and carefully placed it on the smoothing sheet. Craig lowered the upper bladder onto the hot plastic while turning the vacuum pump on. Everyone breathed in, like the vacuum, and held their breath. Within seconds the foot shape appeared in the rubber bladder.

"Will it--"

"Are they holding?"

"Their holding!" Glenn called out.

The vacuum kept pumping, the air kept evacuating, the shape stood firm. Glenn reached under the box and felt the lower bladder lifted up into the shape of the pins on the bottom side balancing the force applied by the upper bladder.

"Alright!" Glenn exclaimed.

"Awesome," from the others.

Glenn wiped the sweat from his forehead while Craig grabbed a wet rag and wiped the upper bladder with cold water to help cool the orthotic below.

In a moment, Craig lifted the upper bladder and revealed a beautiful fully formed orthotic sitting on the mold and all he could think about was the smile on the little boys face, the boy with CP.

Figure - Visible Shape of Orthotic through the Upper Bladder. Photo by Jaren Wilkey, Used by Permission

Three weeks later, with the entire machine now complete, the team was ready to demonstrate. It was a formal design review so the customer brought other important people to witness the event including the little boy. In a small auditorium, Bill demonstrated the machine that pushes all the pins into the shape of a foot then Jake and Craig formed an orthotic on the pins while everyone watched.

Glenn sat proud and recalled the challenge and the satisfaction achieved by the team. He looked over at the boy, eyes still gleaming. "I love engineering."

For refreshments? Juice bags for everyone.

Mentor Discussion and Exercises

Glenn, Jake, Craig and Bill are typical of many engineering teams, sometimes working independently, sometimes working together, always working to a common goal of meeting the customers requirements. In this story we get a sense for how important favorable results might be to a customer, how requirements are used to evaluate the solution, how brainstorming and concept generation are critical to obtaining a better solution, a solution more elegant than previously thought possible.

1. How did this team as a whole react to a major problem?
2. How did each team member react?
3. Would you say that Jake was a good leader?
4. How would you have led the team through this crises?

Creativity and innovation in engineering are fascinating. During most of the story and months before, the team was focused on a particular approach to hold the pins in place. They were trying to rely on friction. Their paradigm was fixed and they spent a lot of time trying to improve that method.

5. What events led them to see things differently?
6. What did they change, where did they go?
7. How could they have made this change in

perspective sooner?

8. It seems that the team made a fundamental omission early in their project. What was it?

They had a friction concept, but it appears that they did not use their academic analysis skills to sum the forces acting on the pins to determine if there was a net force that would cause movement. Such an analysis, months earlier, might have saved some time and effort.

Even so, each team member learned that problem solving in engineering can be challenging and satisfying.

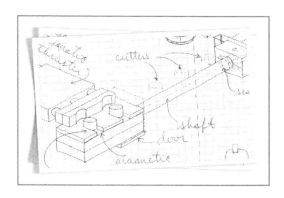

5 - CUTTING EDGE - A CAPSTONE PRIMER

Part 1 – Meet the Team

"Dad, where does gasoline come from?" Aaron said as father and son knelt on the ground filling Aaron's new World War II fighter model airplane with fuel.

"Well, they make it from oil that comes from deep in the earth."

Aaron looked at the ground, then scooped up a little dirt between his thumb and index finger. "How far?"

"Oh, I'd say this much fuel should make the Mustang fly for about ten minutes depending on..."

"No, I mean, how far down in the earth is the oil?" Aaron rubbed his fingers back and forth as the dirt fell back to the earth.

"Oh, a few miles I suppose, longer than a runway at a big airport, except straight down."

Looking down the fuel tube, Aaron carefully replaced the cap while his dad held the plane. "That's a really deep hole," he thought to himself then asked, "But, how do they get to it, and get it out of the ground?"

"They drill a hole and use pumps." Aaron's father smiled, looked his son in the eye, and wiped a few drips from around the engine.

"How do they drill a hole that deep? My earth science teacher told us about the different layers of rock as you go down."

"Well, they use something harder than rock, like diamonds on a big drill bit that turns while it's forced down, you know, like my drill press back at the house, in the corner of the garage, only bigger."

Aaron raised one eye brow.

Aaron's father carefully put the plane on the ground, drew a circle in the dirt about six inches in diameter and said, "Here is the drill bit." Then he poked little holes inside the circle with his index finger. "And here are the diamonds."

Aaron heard a loud horn honk, bringing him back from daydreaming about his father when he was thirteen. The traffic light in front of him was green so he stepped on the gas. Now, as a senior in college and Capstone senior project leader, Aaron and his team mates were on their way to help a company improve their process for making synthetic diamonds for drilling. "I can't believe they asked me to lead this team," he thought. "I can't tell people what to do. I'd rather just be a member of the team, ask lots of questions, get my assignments done, and get a good grade."

"Did everyone remember their notebooks," Aaron said, driving the blue university van with a number 9 on the back.

Each answered yes.

"Guys, I'm a little nervous." Kate said.

"Me too." Aaron thought.

Kate, a manufacturing engineer, lifted her hand from the left armrest leaving finger impressions as she pulled her long dark hair from in front of her face revealing her bright, but cautious smile. "I mean, I feel ready after all those classes on automation, lean-plus, and business, but this is really my first chance to apply it. What if I..."

"I can't wait." Bryce, a mechanical engineer sat just behind Kate leaning inboard anxiously looking past her through the windshield. "I've been working as an intern the last two summers following other engineers around and designing small parts. With this project we'll get to design a whole machine from the ground up."

Aaron listened and reflected on his team. "I'm sure Kate will relax once we find out what we're doing. I'm glad Bryce has experience working in industry."

Aaron looked at Bryce through the rear view mirror making note of his short, sandy blonde hair, sporting a little curl in the front.

Aaron, Kate, and Bryce, along with one other team member, Ray competed for this project on the first week of school. They got the good news yesterday. All in their fourth year of college, they now had the opportunity to apply their skills to a real project, for a real company.

"Remember Kate," Ray leaned forward against his seat belt from the other back seat, "When we wrote our proposal, you were the one who talked us in to bidding for this project."

Kate took a deep breath and raised and lowered her shoulders.

"You liked it," Ray continued, "because it includes automation and probably some software."

"Ray is going to be our team cheerleader," Aaron thought.

"We can do it," Ray added. "I know we can." Ray reached forward, and tapped Kate on the shoulder. "You'll be fine."

Now Aaron could see Ray in the mirror, pleasing smile, brown hair, long sideburns.

"Our objective on this first visit," Aaron said, "is to learn the existing company process and figure out all their needs for this new machine. We are meeting with a guy named,..." Aaron gripped the steering wheel with his left hand and reached in his shirt pocket with his right and pulled out a torn slip of paper. "A guy named, Matt Clawson. Be thinking about your individual expertise and be ready to ask lots of questions from your perspective."

Just a mile away from their destination, Aaron could still see in his mind the six inch circle his father drew in the dirt years ago.

"But who would use real diamonds to dig a hole?" Aaron had asked his father. "Aren't they valuable and expensive and hard to find?"

"They use man made diamonds to do it." Aaron's father said.

"No Way!" Aaron had exclaimed. "I remember my teacher telling us that diamonds form over millions of years deep in the ground with the weight of the earth pushing down on them. The reason we find them is because volcanos bring them to the surface."

"Well, someone has figured out how to do it faster," his father said, "simulating the environment with very high pressure and heat."

Aaron and his father took the model fighter to the large field behind their home, checked all the flaps and settings, then Aaron held the plane while his father flipped the propeller three times. It started. Aaron remembered the very loud buzzing sound.

"What do they make the diamonds out of?" Aaron yelled.

Amidst the high pitched motor noise, Aaron heard his father call back, "I think that would be a good question for your science teacher."

"I don't think he knew the answer," Aaron thought, "but he sure encouraged me to find out.

Part 2 – Meet the Customer

The blue van pulled into the parking lot at HTP Diamond where their Capstone coach, Wesley was waiting.

"I wonder," Bryce said to the team, "if our coach has any experience with synthetic diamonds."

Aaron replied, "I hear he has designed a lot of machines."

"He seemed kind of quiet the other day when we met." Kate added.

Wesley, a middle-aged man, brown hair, six-foot tall and a professional disposition, greeted the team in the parking lot. "Are you ready everyone? This will be a great experience." Wesley turned to Aaron and gave a few words of advice.

In the reception area, they toured the room, drawn toward pictures of oil rigs, drill bits, and photos of employees wearing hard hats and safety glasses.

Aaron walked over to a chromium framed, glass display case in the corner of the room, light reflecting from various shapes and sizes of small metal objects displayed like jewels on black felt. "I remember seeing these."

"Here they are." Aaron turned to the others while pointing at the case. "Remember, we saw some of these on their website. I think these are the diamond cutters."

"What, they use these to cut the diamonds?" Bryce said, hands folded behind his back.

"Is he serious?" Aaron thought then responded "no,

they are cutters *made* out of diamonds, synthetic diamonds."

"They don't look like diamonds."

The team crowded around the case and examined the precious objects, cylindrical like bullets, shiny on the sides, some with flat ends and others rounded with a grey matt finish.

"Welcome."

A young man, about age twenty-five and dark hair, entered the reception area from a door opposite the display case. He held a pair of safety glasses in one hand, and a cell phone in the other.

"I'm Matt Clawson. I'll be your liaison here at HTP Diamond."

"He looks about our age," Aaron thought. "I'm glad to know they hire young engineers. Maybe there'll be an opportunity when we're done. I wonder what HTP stands for."

The coach introduced each team member to Matt.

"We're excited to have you here. The work we need you to do has been on our list for some time, but first, I'd like to take you on a tour and give you an overview of the company and what we do here. You'll each need these."

Matt pointed at several safety glasses sitting on the counter and a box with little bags containing round orange sponges, and then led them down a narrow hallway, walls decorated with numerous framed patents. Matt stopped at another display case and explained the idea of a synthetic diamond cutter, generally small cylindrical metal looking objects that are mounted into larger tools called drill bits.

"Oh, that's what my dad was talking about." Aaron thought, remembering the small drill press in his garage and the six-inch circle in the dirt.

"We produce polycrystalline diamond cutters like these, also known as PDCs or inserts." Matt pointed to several cylindrical objects ranging in size from a lipstick cap to a soda bottle cap. "And we sell them to drill bit manufacturers who then install them into their bits and in turn sell them to oil drilling operators."

"I better write this down," Aaron thought. Each team member opened their notebook and began to write making certain to capture everything they could about the product and the process.

Like ducklings in line behind their mother, the team followed Matt as he led them into the factory where rows of operators were busy at work benches just outside large brick rooms. There was a red and green light above each metal door. Some were illuminated.

"We are dedicated to the highest quality of manufacturing, and our customers expect it. They come to us because they know our cutters will survive miles below the surface under the most demanding environments."

"Hi Jared." Matt turned to a dusty blonde haired man in a white lab coat. "This is the engineering team that is going to look at automating the cutter cleaning operation."

Aaron almost spoke out loud. "Cleaning operation? Did he say we are going to automate a cleaning operation? That doesn't sound very exciting."

With dry cracked hands, Jared handed Matt a small clear plastic storage case from a shelf on the workbench. Matt carefully opened the lid and removed some objects explaining how synthetic diamonds are made. He retrieved several more items from the shelf and laid them in front of the team.

"This is going to be good," Aaron thought.

"We start with premium saw-grade diamond crystals, sintered together at about 1400 C and about 60 kbar, bonded to a tungsten carbide..."

Aaron rubbed the back of his neck with four fingers. "Saw-grade diamond crystals?" Aaron thought. "Sintered? I wonder what that means. I have no idea how much pressure 60 kbar is."

Matt stopped when he saw four straining faces.

Aaron noticed Bryce on his digital device using a units conversion app.

"You can get those details on our website." Matt continued, a little slower this time. "For now, here's the basic process."

"First, we partially fill two or three of these small silver-gray cans with polycrystalline powder like this." Matt demonstrated with Jared's help. "We then insert a tungsten carbide cylinder into the can on top of the powder. Then we stack them up in sets of two or three, separated by discs made of salt into a cube like this." Matt held the assembly between his fingers and slowly moved it horizontally in front of each team member. "Then we put it in the press."

Matt led the team into the nearest metal room; the indicator light was green. The room was nearly *filled* with a large apparatus that looked like six rocket ships pointed nose to nose, having very large cylindrical parts axially aligned towards the center of the room. All surfaces in the room were covered with a fine white dust, a chalk smell filled the air. The room was a little warmer than the main factory.

"This is the press." Matt said. "We have ten of them."

Working with Jared, Matt used a long bar with a forked end to place the cube into the epicenter of the press and again explained that heat and pressure would be applied at 1400 degrees C and about 60 kbar to sinter the materials.

"What does sinter mean?" Bryce whispered to Ray.

Kate leaned over, "I think it means to make it into a solid."

We then exited the room and Jared closed the door. Matt stepped to a control panel and pressed a couple buttons. The light turned red. A loud clanking sound came from the door latch, then the whining of a pump or motor penetrated the walls from somewhere. A minute later the motor stopped and the light returned to green. Matt put on some gloves and led us back into the room. The mist and odor was heavier than before. Using the gloves and fork, Matt removed the cube which was several times smaller than it was before.

"Imagine five armored trucks stacked on your little toe!" Jared said, leaning toward the team.

Ray raised an eyebrow; Kate squinted.

"Thats how much pressure was on the cube."

"High Temperature and High Pressure," Aaron thought.

"Oh I get it." Aaron blurted out. "HTP stands for High Temperature and Pressure, right?"

Matt confirmed Aaron's hypothesis while the team gathered around the work bench where without warning, Matt took a mallet and abruptly smashed the cube and broke it into several pieces. The salt material scattered on the workbench revealing the new, much smaller silver-gray canister containing the new diamonds.

"This is a synthetic diamond." Matt pointed to one of the small dirty cylinders, then tapped it carefully with his bare finger tip.

"It doesn't look like diamond." Jesse said. "Does it ever become clear?"

"No. When finished they will look like polished metal, like the ones in the display case. Before we perform final machining and grinding to our customers specifications, the silver-gray canister material must be removed. It is bonded to the diamond." Matt pointed to a new canister on the shelf reminding them of its purpose to hold and shape the powder until it was made into a diamond.

The team watched and made notes as Matt pressed several new cutters up-side-down into a rubber holder with holes. "A couple of you didn't put in your hearing protection."

"Oh Yah," Aaron remembered.

Matt then took us to a small closet between two press rooms.

"To remove the silver-gray canister material, we blast the cutter with high velocity Silicon Carbide (SiC) grit very much like sandblasting but the SiC is highly abrasive. It'l remove everything, except the diamond."

Part 3 – Experience The Product

In the small room stood a filthy laboratory-looking cabinet with a cloudy viewport above two round hand-size holes. Matt opened the window and put the new cutters inside then closed the window and reached in through the two round holes. Each hole was fitted with a rubber glove reaching inside the machine where the operator could insert hands and arms, hold the objects inside of the cabinet, and perform the blasting operation. Jared demonstrated. Everyone covered their ears.

Aaron thought, "Now I know what the orange sponges are for." He pushed the earplugs into his ears.

Each team member was given the opportunity to look through the window to see what Jared was doing. With cutters in one hand, and a blasting nozzle at the end of a hose in the other hand, Aaron, Bryce, Kate, and Ray pretended they could see what was going on, but the dust was too thick. As Jared worked, a very loud hissing sound emanated from the nozzle inside the cabinet.

"Boy," Aaron thought. "I would hate to work in this environment every day for hours. No wonder Jared's hands are all cracked. I wonder if he's really blonde, or if that's polychristalin powder in his hair."

With safety glasses, ear plugs and respirator, using back and forth motions, Jared took half a minute to blast or clean the can material from several cutters, then turned the machine off and invited us all back to the workbench.

Aaron looked around, seeing similar operations through the factory asked, "How many press stations did you say you have?"

"Ten presently," Matt responded. "We have one blasting cabinet for each press station." Matt put a hand on Jared's shoulder. "Out of all the jobs to do at HTP Diamond, this is the least desirable, and the least healthy. That's why you're here. We need you to automate the blasting process." Matt patted Jared's shoulder. "We would like to free up our operators to work other tasks while the blasting is taking place."

As Matt spoke, Jared nodded in violent agreement.

"Jared, tell'm what it's like in there." Matt said.

Jared removed his safety glasses and respirator leaving a clear mark across his forehead. Below the mark the skin around his eyes was wet, above the line was dirty sweat. "Well, the head gear is hot and bulky, and by the end of the day, your just shaking..." Jared stopped, looked toward the team, then at Matt. "I'll tell you what. Why don't we just have *them* blast the next cutters and they can see for themselves what it's like. It's not very difficult, its just..."

"Perfect." Matt said. "Who would like to go first?"

Bryce opened his mouth to speak but stopped when Kate raised her hand.

Several eyebrows raised.

"I nominate Aaron." Kate said.

Everyone looked at Kate.

"Thanks Kate." Aaron thought.

"Well, you're our leader. And then, I'll go next." Kate said gesturing with both hands, palms up. If we're going to automate this, let's see how it's done.

"Way to go Kate." Ray acknowledged.

"I like her style," Aaron admitted.

Jared handed the respirator to Aaron and gave him some instructions while stretching the elastic band over his head. "Do you have your ear plugs in?"

"Yes," Aaron replied.

Jared inserted a new cutter into the rubber holder and showed Aaron how to hold it.

"I can't see anything with this mask on," Aaron thought.

Jared guided Aaron into the blasting room and without turning on the SiC, walked Aaron through the process then asked if he was ready.

"Yes," Aaron said.

"What did you say," Jared asked.

"Yes," Aaron yelled this time with a distinct nod, then thought, "Ready or not, let's give this a try."

Jared closed the door on the blaster, looked through the window to make sure Aaron had a good grip on the rubber holder and the nozzle, then held his thumb up.

Aaron nodded again.

Jared turned on the SiC blaster, a very loud hissing sound filled the room and immediately the nozzle lifted Aaron's hand upward.

"Wo," Aaron thought, "this thing has thrust; Houston, we have lift-off."

The nozzle vibrated in Aaron's hand, the cabinet filling with dust as thick as fog. "I can't see anything." Aaron said but know one could hear him. "Where's the cutter? I hope I don't blast through the glove."

Trying to hold the cutter and focus the nozzle on the cutter was hard enough, but looking through the helmet glass and the cabinet window made it even harder. Aaron shuffled his feet for balance, and adjusted his posture to get a better view then with imagination, aimed the nozzle directly toward the top of the cutter. It glowed white as canister material heated and eroded from the surface of the cutter. The light penetrated the mist like a automobile headlight through dense fog on a cold winter day, bright in the center, then fading outward. After several seconds the can material was gone from one edge of the cutter so Aaron slowly aimed the nozzle more toward the center. Eventually the glowing stopped. "I guess that means all the niobium is gone."

Jared watched through the cabinet window and turned the blasting system off.

"My hands are so sweaty and shaking. These gloves are hot."

"Okay Kate, its your turn." Aaron said as he peeled the respirator from his face.

As Kate and the others took their turn, Aaron imagined the hours and hours that Jared and his co-workers had spent with this hot space-suit on.

"I hope we can fix this," Aaron thought. "We've got to make a machine that will automate this process and improve life for these operators. What if we fail? How are we going to create a machine that will hold the cutters and nozzle, move them around, and sense when the niobium is gone?"

Part 4 – Uncover Customer Needs

Wesley, the team Coach was the last one in the booth. After the blasting experience, Matt took the sweaty team to see the machining processes performed after blasting, then led them to a conference room where they found a large table, several employees, and a whiteboard on the wall. Fortunately, there was a box of tissues on the table.

Wesley gathered the team briefly for a huddle in the corner of the room. "Remember, all team members should take good notes during this conversation. Ask lots of questions, and listen to everything they have to say. Our goal is to take this information and write specifications for the machine. By the way, I noticed Bryce sketching what was going on out in the shop.

Good job Bryce."

"Okay," Matt began. "Now you know what Jared and all our blasting operators go through to get these cutters clean."

Wesley wiped his forehead and nodded for Aaron to take over.

"That was very eye opening," Aaron said. "Before we as a team get serious about design options, we need to come to some agreement on specifications for the machine, and to do that, we'd like to ask a few questions."

Matt introduced the employees from HTP Diamond in the room and stated what their specialties are, and then Aaron had each team member introduce themselves.

"Well, let's start with Jared," Matt said. "Tell the team what the machine needs to do from your perspective."

"Do you mind if we capture these on the whiteboard?" Aaron asked.

"No problem."

"Kate, would you be our scribe today?"

"Well," Jared began, "First and foremost the machine needs to remove the silver-gray canister material from the bottom of the cutter without any operator interaction. I want to walk up to the machine, insert a cutter, press a button, then when I return, the cutter needs to be clean, or blasted ready for me to pick it up and install the next cutter."

Kate stopped writing on the whiteboard for a moment and asked, "What is the required cycle time?"

"Oh, I think 15 seconds per cutter is about right, unless you find a way to blast faster. Right now it takes about 15 seconds to blast each cutter then move to the next cutter in the holder."

"Can the machine blast more than one cutter at a time?" Ray said.

"I don't see why not as long as the average time is 15 seconds per cutter. The next thing is that the machine needs to recycle the grit for multiple uses. Right now we have to move the grit from a container down below the machine, examine it to see if it can be used again, and if it can, move it up into the hopper for re-use. It's an activity we would like automated."

"So, some kind of recirculation system to cycle and check the grit?" Bryce asked. "How long does the grit last; how much grit is used to blast a certain number of cutters?"

"That all depends," Jared said, "on the hardness of the can, the age of the grit and other factors. I'd suggest you do some testing to determine that. Matt, can we give them some samples to test?"

"Absolutely."

Each team member continued to make notes while Kate wrote on the board.

"Anything else Jared?" Matt said.

"Oh yes, if you handle more than one cutter at a time, and especially if you drop them into a bin when your done, remember, they can't touch each other. The diamond from one cutter will damage another cutter if they come in contact." Jared waited while the team wrote this down. "And one more thing, we don't want to have to use a tool to press the cutters out of a holder like we do now. We would like the cutters to be free, perhaps in a bin of cooling water, ready to be picked up by hand and placed on the polishing machine."

"What is the polishing machine?" Kate asked.

"Oh, it's that rotary device we showed you right next to the blasting table that has holes or receptacles for many cutters. It laps the surface of the cutter against a fine stone."

Matt moved the meeting forward. "Okay, Jared, we'll come back to you in a few minutes to see if you have any more needs. Let's go next to Peter, our safety representative."

"I can imagine," Aaron thought, "that he's going to have a lot of requirements."

"All of our machines need to conform to regulatory requirements to protect the operators and others near the machines. Instead of listing each one right now, I will email the list to you. Let me just emphasize that the machine will need provisions for protecting employees from electric shock and accidental contact with harmful forces, pressures, fluids, etc. If the machine has any actuators or motors, and it sounds like this one will, there will need to be two buttons for the operator to push simultaneously to start the operation cycle,..."

"Why two start buttons," Aaron wondered.

Kate asked, "Why two start buttons?"

"So both hands of the operator are definitely out of harms way."

"Oh yah." Kate said. "I knew that."

"And also an emergency stop button to immediately disconnect all power and stop all motion. Look at our other machines and you can see how this is done."

"That reminds me," Jared said, "We don't want to have to wear extra hearing protection, so we want the machine to have acoustic coverings to keep the sound below the safety requirement."

"And that reminds me," Peter added, "That the machine needs to capture the Silicon Carbide dust; their can't be any grit floating in the air to get into people's lungs."

This process continued as the representatives from maintenance and automation spoke their needs and the team wrote diligently.

"Now then," Matt said to the team members, "Do you have any questions for us about the machine?"

"Yes. Kate, why don't you go first?" Aaron said.

"Okay. One of my specialties is software." Kate rubbed her nose. "Well, at least I've had a couple classes. What kind of controller and software do you want us to use?"

"We use PLCs (programmable-logic-controllers) and modern latter-logic software, so we would like you to be consistent with what we already have. That way our programmers can make adjustments in the future. I'll send you a link to the specific PLC company."

"How many variations of cutters are you going to

use on this machine?" Kate continued. "Will the software need to consider different cases for different variations?

Jared and Matt looked at each other.

"Excellent question," Aaron thought.

"Well," Matt said, "Our cutters range in diameter from 15 to 25 millimeters, so..."

"And the larger ones take longer to be blasted." Jared added.

"So for now," Matt continued, "let's say that we will need to handle different diameters in that range, and we will have to determine how this affects the software."

Each team member took turns asking questions for another hour whereupon the rate of questions decreased to where it was obvious the team had enough information to at least get started.

Looking at Wesley for concurrence, Matt brought the meeting to an end. Wesley nodded to Aaron.

Leaving the room Aaron said. "We will meet as a team now and digest all that we've learned and begin to put this information into solid specific requirements for you to review. Thanks everyone for being such great hosts today."

Matt and the team bid their good-byes and headed back to the van sharing their individual experiences in the hot gloves.

Part 5 – Refine the Specifications

"How are we ever going to make sense of all this?"

Bryce admitted the next day at school. "I don't see how we can get our arms around all these requirements."

"He's right," Aaron thought. "We've got information in log books, lap top files, website printouts. How do we get this organized? What do I do to keep my team moving forward? And where is Ray?"

"Okay," Aaron said. "Let's get these into one place or one document so we can group them."

The team, less Ray, began compiling customer needs, grouping them into categories such as cutter handling, machine operation, versatility, safety, maintenance, control system and mechanical. They reviewed other requirements found on the company's website and studied the safety and regulatory requirements sent by Peter.

"Ray, we're glad you could join us." Bryce said as Ray came in a half hour late.

"Well, now that we have them divided into categories," Aaron assured, "let's look for overlaps or similarities, get rid of duplicates, then create a clean list."

"How about if we prioritize each one, say on a scale of one to three," Ray suggested. "We could just put one, two, or three asterisks by each item. That will help us focus."

The team worked diligently for several days reading, discussing and adjusting the customer needs statements until they felt they were ready to start extracting succinct requirements statements upon which they could apply metrics. Occasionally a sketch or two was drawn to discuss possible solutions but that was premature. At this stage it was time to focus on the 'Whats', not the 'Hows.' At last, the Specification began to emerge.

Another thing that emerged was a machine name. At first, as they conversed with each other, referring to the yet uncreated machine, they used terms like blaster, diamond blaster, automated blasting machine, and others. Eventually, realizing they were all using different terminology in their conversations, they got their heads together and debated options for the name of the machine. They eventually converged on AutoBlaster, or AB, short for Automated Diamond Blaster.

By way of phone calls, teleconferences and face to face meetings, the team met with the customer several times to discuss and adjust the requirements before all agreed as follows.

- *The AutoBlaster shall remove 100% of the silver-gray canister material from the flat surface of the cutter*
- *The AutoBlaster shall not blast or damage the cylindrical sides of the cutter*
- *Averaged over a batch of cutters, the AutoBlaster shall remove can material in 30 seconds maximum (20 seconds ideal)*
- *The AutoBlaster shall receive one or more cutters from an operator and begin the blasting cycle when the operator presses two start buttons*
- *The AutoBlaster shall blast cutters of any diameter between 15 and 25 millimeters*
- *The AutoBlaster shall not allow cutters to physically contact each other*

- *The AutoBlaster shall operate continuously for two shifts per day (16 hours), 6 days per week, 3 months without the need for preventative maintenance.*
- *The AutoBlaster shall have a mean time between failure (MTBF) of 10,000 hours.*
- *Where feasible, the AutoBlaster shall use components consistent with other similar machines at HTP.*
- *The AutoBlaster shall comply with OSHA (Occupational Safety and Health Administration) requirements*
- *At a distance of 3 feet or greater from the AutoBlaster, at any time during operation, the AutoBlaster noise shall not exceed requirements specified in OSHA 1910.95.*
- *SiC escape from the AutoBlaster shall comply with OSHA requirements*
- *The AutoBlaster shall be mobile by lockable wheels installed on the machine. Two of the four casters shall be swivel type.*
- *The AutoBlaster user interface shall consist of simple buttons, switches or dials. [The AutoBlaster shall not require a Graphical User Interface (GUI)].*
- *The AutoBlaster shall include a 'light' pole providing operator visual indication of machine status including 'In Operation', 'Ready', or 'Fault'.*
- *The AutoBlaster shall cost less than $30,000 per unit to produce a quantity of 10 units. (The team shall produce one fully functional prototype).*
- *The AutoBlaster shall be delivered and fully tested by March 30th.*

Aaron made a personal trip back to HTP Diamond to get Matt's signature on the Specification sheet. "Now at least we know for sure 'what' the machine has to do to please the customer," Aaron thought. "I'm not too worried about their cost requirement, and I think working smart as a team, we can find or develop the technology that's needed, well, at least Wesley thinks we can. But I don't know how we are going to get it all done, ready for testing, in a little over six months."

Part 6 – Compose the Functions

"Aaron, I can't wait to show you what I've done."

"Who is this?" Aaron spoke into the phone.

"It's Ray. I can't wait to show you the Functional Decomposition."

"The what?"

"The Functional Decomposition, you know, for the machine. I was so excited about the project I did it over the weekend. I hope you don't mind."

"Sounds great." Aaron said. "Gee, thanks. Let's have you go first on the agenda at our meeting tomorrow morning."

"Okay, I'll see you then. Eight o'clock sharp." Aaron said.

"Was that really Ray?" Aaron thought. "That will be a first if he's on time."

Aaron arrived early to get the room ready but Ray beat him to it. All four team members were on time ready to go. Ray was bouncing with excitement so Aaron made no delay.

Ray began, "I started by thinking through the sequence our machine will need to go through. Then I wrote the sequence steps from the perspective of the machine."

"The machine doesn't have a perspective," Bryce said.

The door opened and in walked Wesley. "Hey, could you use an extra team member today?"

Ray made a fist with his right hand, thrust it forward a little and under his breath cheered, "Yes!"

"You bet," Aaron said. "We appreciate any ideas you have. It seems that Ray was doing some deep thinking over the weekend."

"Great," Wesley responded. "Please keep going."

Bryce repeated to Ray, "You make the machine sound like it can think."

"Well, it will have a programmable controller, so I guess you could say it can think. Look at it this way, the controller doesn't know anything except what it senses by way of inputs like sensors and switches."

"That's right," Kate said. "We learned all about that in my automation class. Controllers have inputs and outputs, or I/O for short."

Ray continued, "The inputs will allow the controller to know the state of the machine so it can take action steps and perform functions or outputs. Here are the actions, and then I will show you what I recommend for functions."

"Boy I'm glad he's on our team," Aaron thought. "I hope Kate doesn't mind Ray working in her territory."

Ray moved to the whiteboard. "First the machine needs to 'Receive and Retain two cutters."

"Wait a minute," Bryce interrupted. "The specification says 'one or more cutters.'"

"I know, but for discussion purposes, let's suppose the number of cutters is two. I noticed the other day that many of their batches are done in twos. This assumption will let us move forward in Functional Decomposition. Next, the machine needs to wait for and 'Receive a Start indication' from the operator."

"Two start indications." Kate reminded.

Ray continued step by step writing the generic machine sequence on the left side of the board, explaining his thoughts whenever a question was asked. Wesley added a little here and there, but generally sat in his chair nodding his head with a proud smile.

"Here are the steps of a machine cycle from beginning to end."

1. Receive and Retain two cutters
2. Receive Start indications
3. Detect operator safety clearance
4. Move first cutter into position for blasting
5. Seal enclosure
6. Start blasting and blasting timer
7. Wait for timer to expire
8. Stop blasting
9. Move second cutter into position for blasting
10. (Repeat 6-8)
11. Open enclosure
12. Move cutters to pickup position
13. Release cutters

14. Reset all elements of the machine

"I've looked over this list several times and have decomposed the basic machine functions as follows." Ray looked hopeful toward his bright-eyed team mates as he began writing on the right side of the board. "Essentially, we need to design a machine that will do these things."

1. Receive and Retain Two Cutters
2. Move Cutters to Multiple Positions
3. Provide a Containment Environment that can be opened
4. Perform directed SiC Blasting and SiC recovery
5. Provide operator Interface with Start, Stop, and Options Selection
6. Provide Control System with Controller, Electrical, and Software
7. Provide Machine Structure, Cabinet, misc

"I think you missed one." Kate said.

Everyone looked at Kate, then turned to Ray, and then back to Kate."

"Hang in there Ray," Aaron thought. "I was hoping Kate or Bryce would speak up."

"I know it's kind of general," Kate said, "but the machine needs functionality for interfacing with it's surroundings."

"What do you mean?" Aaron asked.

"Well, the machine will likely need electrical power,

perhaps compressed air, and maybe a ventilation system."

Everyone looked at Wesley who pressed his lips together and gave a favorable nod.

"Okay," Ray said turning back to Kate. "What would you like to call that function?"

"How about, 'Physical and Electrical Interfaces,' or something like that?"

Ray added it to the board.

8. Provide Physical and Electrical Interfaces (e.g. power, air, ventilation)

"Does anyone have any more functions to add?" Ray asked.

"Well," Aaron said, "I think this looks pretty great. Thanks Ray. What made you think of this anyway?"

"Oh," Ray looked over at Wesley who remained silent. "I was working on my motorcycle Saturday and I got to thinking about it's different parts, and I started thinking about the functions each part or assembly performs. Like, the brake handles, cables, and calipers perform the stopping function, the motor and throttle perform the acceleration function, the wheels, bearings and tires perform the rolling and steering function, the bike frame..."

"We get the idea," Aaron said.

"Anyway," Ray continued, "When designing something new, you just reverse the process by determining the functions that are needed, and then you can figure out what parts you need to accomplish those functions. I did it for the AutoBlaster by starting with the sequence, then figuring out the functions needed for that sequence."

"I'm gonna start doing more of that kind of thinking when I look at things." Aaron said.

"Don't do it at the dinner table," Kate said. "Your wife might not be interested in what function the tables and chairs perform."

"Good job Ray," Bryce added.

"Yes, great job everyone." Wesley leaned forward looking one by one at each team member in the eye. "You are making great progress and I can tell you are each being proactive. Before we go any further, we need to go visit some places that have machines that do these kind of things, these functions. Matt, from HTP Diamond has arranged for us to visit a company not too far from them that uses sand-blasting in their production of jewelry and metal medallions. Our machine will be doing a kind of sand-blasting, and it will be handling small objects about the size of jewelry.

"That sounds awesome," Bryce said. "What's it called?"

"Recognition Services Incorporated, or RSI."

"Bryce, would you arrange the van again?" Aaron said.

"In the mean time," Wesley added, "every chance you get, open your notebooks and brainstorm ideas for accomplishing these functions. Look at everything around you and see if you can see things that hold or clamp parts, that move parts from one point to another. Keep your list of functions handy and look for existing machines, devices, objects, at home, at work, everywhere."

Part 7 – Go Benchmarking

"Can you believe it?" Kate spoke lightly to Bryce. "Look at this place. The whole factory is carpeted, even under the machines."

The team followed Rex Morgan into the automation area at Recognition Services Incorporated. Equipment was arranged generally in several lines so that raw materials passed from one end of the line to the other being stamped, formed, engraved, and cleaned before being received by an operator at the other end.

"This is so impressive," Aaron thought. "I wonder who designs all this equipment. Do they buy it, or make it themselves. And the people look like they enjoy working here."

"Mr. Morgan," Aaron asked. "Do you design these machines in house, or contract with other companies to make them?"

"We make all our own tooling, the dies, the cutters, things like that. We also design and make many of the machines. We have a very talented team of engineers and designers. Some of the standard equipment, we buy complete, but we work close with our automation suppliers whether we're buying a complete machine, or just components."

Soon the team was standing around a small table with two white vertical PVC pipe assemblies side-by-side on the top, and flexible hosing coming out the bottom. There were two antenna looking devices on the front two corners of the table, a large red button in the center, and blue flexible tubing coming out the top of each PVC assembly.

"I recognize this." Bryce said.

"What is your name again?" Rex asked.

"Bryce."

"Go ahead Bryce. Tell us what you see."

"Well, it looks like you open the cap on the front and put small parts in the little tray to be sand-blasted. Then you close the door... No, it looks like the little door automatically closes when the tray is pulled inside."

"Thats right."

"So when the machine starts..." Bryce walked around to the back of the PVC assembly. "So when the machine starts, this piston or cylinder back here pulls the tray inside the blasting area and the spring loaded door closes automatically. Then the blasting starts. It looks like the sand comes through this blue tube up here, then.." Bryce bent over and looked under the table. "Then the sand and air is collected through these large hoses and fed back to the source." Bryce pointed behind the blasting table to what appeared to be a sand blasting supply and recovery system.

"Wow," Aaron thought, "this looks like exactly what we need, except I bet you can't use SiC in this blaster, the PVC would probably be destroyed."

Ray and Kate were moving all around the machine to get a better view of all its gadgets.

"How long does it take?" Ray asked. "I mean, what do you blast with this machine, and how long does it take to..."

"We sand-blast our medallions for example, to remove the burrs and residue created during our various processes. Typically, the blasting takes less than a minute."

"How loud is it?" Kate said while looking down the row at an operator wearing ear plugs on a nearby blasting station.

"We've measured the noise to be... Well I don't know the decibels off-hand but it exceeds OSHA requirements so our operators need to wear extra hearing protection. I have an engineer looking into ways that we could reduce the noise level."

Team members asked more questions regarding the blasting nozzles, tubing materials, maintenance requirements, type of controller and software.

"Seeing this blaster has been great." Ray said. "I think a concept like this would work well at HTP Diamond except..."

"Except for the PVC." Bryce said. "There's no way it would stand up to the SiC."

"Yeh," Ray continued. "That's what I was going to say. But I think it could be done with a different material, I mean, the enclosure could be something much harder."

"Mr. Morgan?" Kate asked. "Can you show us

inside the control box? I'd like to see the PLC."

Rex gave the team a thorough view of the inside and outside of the machine, then escorted them to a small conference room where he addressed remaining questions.

"Rex," Wesley asked when team member questions were exhausted, "These engineering students will be graduating soon and we want them to be leaders in their profession. Leaders in academic skills, leaders in finding solutions to help the world, and leaders in people skills. What do you expect from your engineers at RSI?"

Aaron thought, "I was hoping he would ask that question."

"I was hoping someone would ask that question." Rex said.

"Hey, thats exactly what I was thinking." Aaron thought.

Rex walked over to a framed, glass covered plaque on the wall and lifted it off it's hook. "Here is what we expect of our engineers and designers." Rex passed the list around.

"It must be important to be hanging on the wall of the conference room." Aaron thought.

"We expect them to have a good foundation and working ability in the tools we use like CAD and PLC programming. They need an understanding of mechanical tolerances, and materials used in machine design. They need to be good trouble-shooters, good problem solvers to keep the machines running. You need an understanding of pneumatics and electro-mechanical devices like cylinders and valves. And it is very important that you understand quality control practices like SPC and Lean."

"Statistical Process Control, right?" Kate said.

"Right."

"What about Personal or Interpersonal Skills?" Aaron asked.

"Oh absolutely. Product Development can be stressful and it always involves many people like co-workers, management, operators, maintenance, customers, suppliers... You need to be able to work with all these people collaboratively, constructively and respectfully. In fact, we've learned that the best solutions come from involving all these people. Never work in isolation."

"Anything else?" Wesley said.

"Yes, Rex continued, "you should get in the habit of being creative, drawing sketches of your ideas, building prototypes, being self-motivated and persistent, and it wouldn't hurt to have an understanding of electrical wiring, power supplies, relays and those kinds of things."

Part 8 – Sketch Many Concepts

"That trip to RSI yesterday was great," Bryce said.

"Yah!" Ray agreed. "You know, I think our machine could be very similar to their sand-blaster. We just need to make it more of a tank so it can stand the SiC."

Kate added her thoughts. "And our machine needs to process probably a lot more parts and not wear out. RSI doesn't use the machine continuously like HTP Diamond will be using their blaster, I mean AutoBlaster."

Aaron called the group to order.

"Okay, I hope each of you have been thinking of concepts for the various functions of the machine."

"Why are we meeting in a classroom today, and at 2 p.m.?" Bryce asked.

Aaron pointed at the wall-to-wall whiteboard at the head of the class. "So we could all use the whiteboard at the same time and immediately see each others concepts. Most of the rooms are booked all morning starting at eight." Aaron pulled some loose sheets of paper from his notebook. "Wesley couldn't meet with us today, but as you will see in a minute, he did a lot of thinking and sketching overnight. He scanned and emailed his sketches and I printed them this morning."

"Let's review our Functional Decomposition, thanks again Ray, then get started with our group brainstorm session. I wrote them on this poster to put beside the whiteboard to remind us. I propose that we focus today on the functions that involve moving parts. That's the first three on our list."

1. Receive and Retain Two Cutters
2. Move Cutters to Multiple Positions
3. Provide a Containment Environment that can be opened

4. Perform directed SiC Blasting and SiC recovery
5. Provide operator Interface with Start, Stop, and Options Selection
6. Provide Control System with Controller, Electrical, and Software
7. Provide Machine Structure, Cabinet, misc
8. Provide Physical and Electrical Interfaces (e.g. power, air, ventilation)

Aaron wrote the three functions across the top of the whiteboard leaving plenty of working space for many concepts. "Work in which ever function you want, there should be enough room for two or three people to work on the same function at the same time if necessary. Sketch whatever you drew in your notebooks, or whatever you think of for the next 20 minutes. This will be a silent brainstorm, no talking, just sketching and writing. Label each of your sketches with a descriptive name. Then we'll take time for each person to explain their concepts and respond to questions. During the first round, there will be no criticism. Then we'll repeat the brainstorm again, this time allowing comments. Let's get started."

"Hey," Bryce immediately broke the silence rule. "This blue pen doesn't work."

"Just get another one."

"Don't put it back on the tray," Ray demanded. "Throw it in the trash can. I hate it when people put a bad pen back on the tray for the next guy."

With notebooks or scratch paper in one hand, and dry erase markers in the other, illustrations began to replace the plane white space across the wall. Some sketches were clean and orderly, some looked like they were made by a two year old, but all served a good purpose to get ideas out on the table (or on the whiteboard in this case) and out of the heads of the creative team.

Kate drew a fork or goal post device with a cutter on the top of each vertical post. She then drew a motor or actuator under the goal post and circular arrows indicating that the post can rotate about a vertical axis. Next to the arrows she wrote "180 degrees." She drew what looked like a kitchen faucet spraying down on one of the cutters.

"I'm sorry about my drawings," Kate said. "I never was very..."

"Kate," Aaron said sharply but politely, "No talking."

"What is she talking about," Aaron thought, "her sketches are great compared to mine. In fact, she draws better than the rest of the team."

While the team continued to draw, Aaron taped Wesley's sketches on the board under the functions that seemed applicable. The allotted twenty minutes went by pretty quick.

Part 9 - Explain and Discuss Concepts

"Okay, everybody finish the sketch you're working on

and let's get ready for the next step. Don't worry, this is just the beginning. We'll take a lot more time to brainstorm."

Pen caps returned to pens, and pens returned to the tray.

"Let's start with the first function, 'Receive and Retain' and have each person explain their concept. Hopefully, Wesley's concepts will be self explanatory."

"Kate, please go first."

"Okay, in this concept, the cutters are held in place by magnets, one on each end of a round cylinder. The operator has to orient each cutter with the canister facing away from the magnet, but no action is required by the operator to get the cutters to stay in place. This drawing also shows a concept for movement and enclosure, but I'll wait until we get to those functions."

"Cool." Ray said.

"Good job Kate." Bryce added.

"Okay, Ray, why don't you go next?"

"Mine is similar to Kate's, except the magnet assembly is more complex." Ray pointed at a round thick disc with a large circle in the center and smaller circles around the perimeter. "In the center is a strong electro-magnet that energized to keep the cutter in place while being blasted, you know, to keep it from being blasted off. Then around the circumference of the magnetic assembly, there are a number of weaker magnets that hold the cutter when the operator first puts the cutters in place. In either case, some how the cutters will have to be pulled off or pushed off the magnets when their done."

"Bryce, your turn."

"Down where I work, they use suction cups to hold panels in place. I wonder if something like that could be used to hold the cutters. Anyway, this part in the center is a suction cup." Bryce pointed at a conical figure, something like an ice cream sugar cone, with a flexible tube coming out the bottom. A cylindrical cutter was shown just above the cone. "Their usually made out of some kind of rubber and come in various shapes and sizes. Some of them even have bellows, accordion shapes to allow them to expand and contract easily. The tube coming out the bottom is the vacuum or suction hose. The suction is controlled by some kind of valve which can be turned on and off by the controller. This way, the operator can put the cutter on the gripper or vacuum cup, press a button with the other hand, or maybe step on a foot pedal to cause the vacuum cup to grip the cutter."

"Great job so far. Okay, let's look at Wesley's sketches and see what he had in mind. This first one he called a Double-V with Symmetric Grippers."

"I think Wesley has done this before," Aaron thought. "He labelled all his concepts and listed which function is applicable."

"I think I see how it works." Bryce jumped in. "In the center, there is what machinists call a V-block except this one has two back-to-back Vs, one for each cutter. Then this gripper device below it does a pinching action." Bryce extended his right hand and moved his thumb and fore finger toward and away from each other."

"Here's the note," Aaron said, "that Wesley sent with this sketch. It reads, 'With gripper open, operator inserts two cutters on supports and against V-Blocks. Upon actuation, gripper fingers close and compress cutters against V-Blocks. Periodically replace sacrificial shields.'"

"What does he mean by *sacrificial shields?*" Kate asked.

The team looked closer at Wesley's sketch.

"Look down here, in the middle." Bryce pointed. "It says sacrificial rubber shield, and then there are two arrows pointing to something on top of the V-Block. Oh, that's to protect the V-Block from the SiC. Occasionally as it wears down, you just replace the shield so you won't have to replace the V-block."

"How do you make a gripper like that?" Aaron asked.

"I think you can buy them that way." Bryce said. "Wesley must have some experience with that kind of thing."

"Bryce, can you ask Wesley more about this kind of gripper?"

The team continued through a few more 'Receive and Retain' concepts, then moved on to the 'Move Cutters' function, and then on to the 'Enclosure' function. After several hours, they took photographs of the whiteboard, and decided to called it a day. They had over two dozen concepts from their first brainstorm session.

"Let's meet back here the same time tomorrow and continue our concept generation. I'm sure that between now and then, we'll think of some more possibilities."

"I hope we can move on to the control part soon." Kate said. "I've had some ideas swimming around in my head ever since Ray told us about the machine sequence that led him to the major functions."

For five straight days the team met and re-met covering the whiteboard with new concepts. There were great ideas for how to move the cutters between the inside and outside of the enclosure. They debated whether they should have one or two nozzles, or move the two cutters under the nozzle one at a time for blasting. They discussed the total machine layout, where the blasting unit would go, how the SiC would be recycled from the blasting chamber back to the SiC supply unit. All in all there were more than fifty individual concepts supporting all the functions, and over one hundred various combinations of all the concepts. Their notebooks were getting full. They took photographs of all the whiteboard sketches and posted them on the team website for all to review.

"Now what do we do?" Aaron thought. "We have all these concepts. Several of them are pretty good. Which one do we use? How do we figure out which ones are better than others? We're gonna have to sort out those that aren't as good. We're probably going to hurt some feelings. Everyone needs to be involved. We've got to get the number down to a few. How do we do this? By what criteria do we choose or eliminate?"

Part 10 – Architect the Machine

"Good morning everyone." Aaron said. "Wesley suggested we meet in the lab today so we could use these big tables to spread out our concept sheets and try to group them into practical whole-machines concepts. Ray, would you please help me slide these two tables together?"

"Guys, I'm starting to get worried," Bryce interrupted. "We've got seven months to get a machine ready for testing, we've already used up one month, and we don't even know what were designing yet. Our first informal design review is in two weeks."

"I was afraid of this," Aaron admitted to himself. "It's probably my fault. I haven't been leading fast enough and we're running out of time."

"I think we're making good progress." Ray assured Bryce. "We know what the Requirements are, and we have a list of functions, and now we have all these possible concepts..."

"Yah," Bryce continued, "But how can we possibly narrow it down to one concept, get it designed in CAD, buy or make all the parts, assemble it and test it all in six more months. Some of the parts might take weeks to get. Why don't we get Matt over here and have him tell us which concept he thinks is best?"

"He doesn't know," Ray said. "Thats what he hired

us to do."

"But he is around this kind of equipment every day." Bryce insisted.

"How am I gonna get these two calmed down," Aaron thought. "I have the same worries as Bryce, but I still think if we work together, and work smart, we can get this done."

"I was also thinking," Kate inserted. "That Wesley has a lot of experience. Let's just have him go through the stack of ideas and tell us which ones are more practical."

"Kate," Aaron said. "I'm sure Wesley will participate, but I don't think he's going to make the decisions for us. He's a believer in team work and team inspiration. But if it makes you all feel better, He plans to be here shortly."

Aaron led the team over to the long table and asked everyone to get out all their papers or photographs with concepts.

"I don't have all my concepts on paper." Bryce admitted. "Some of them I drew on my device, and some are on CAD."

"Well, then take some post-it notes and write a phrase describing each concept and give each a name. Don't forget to write the applicable function on the note. To get started, Wesley suggested we put all concepts for each function in a vertical line or column, one concept above the other on the table. For example, all the 'Receive and Retain' function concepts get lined up in the first column, then the next column is for all the 'Move Cutters' function concepts, just like we did last week on the whiteboard when we drew the concepts except this time, we'll make a single row or column of concepts so we should end up with as many columns as we have functions."

"There isn't enough room," Kate noted, "for all the concepts to be placed in a column."

"Aaron," Ray said. "Let's get another two tables and make one large table two high and two wide."

"Some of my sketches apply to more than one function." Kate said.

"Just pick a place under one of the applicable functions. It's okay"

For the next ten minutes the team sorted through their concepts placing them under the applicable function, re-drawing, or re-writing where necessary to get them all in.

"Great," Aaron said. "Now, here's what we do. We each take a marker and…"

"Oh, how could I be so stupid," Aaron thought. "I forgot the butcher paper. I'm gonna have a mutiny on my hands.

Aaron stopped, pressed his lips together, looked toward the end of the room and shrugged his shoulders. "Sorry guys, I forgot to put butcher paper down first. We need to be able to draw arrows from left to right, from column to column, combining concepts into potential whole machines. See that role of butcher paper on the tool crib?"

"These are old work benches," Kate said with a

frown. "Let's just draw on the table."

Everyone looked at Kate with surprised expressions.

"I didn't think the mutiny would start with Kate," Aaron thought.

"Just kidding."

"Kate, you had me worried." Aaron said. "Okay, before we move the papers, let's give each concept a label, like A1, A2, A3,... B1, B2, B3,... and so forth. 'A' is for 'Receive and Retain,' 'B' is for 'Move Cutters,' and so on."

"I'll take care of that." Ray said.

After another ten minutes the concepts were labelled, removed, and then replaced on the table now covered with butcher paper.

"Looks good!" Wesley came into the room holding a box of donuts and gave a funny look at the table configuration.

"I'm saved," Aaron thought.

"Ingenuity I see." Wesley said. "I like that. Wow, I've never seen so many concept papers. You guys are steaming with greatness. I see you remembered the butcher paper. My last team forgot the paper and had to lay out all the concept sheets twice."

Everyone looked at Aaron who immediately put his left index finger vertically in front of his lips and said, "shh."

"I won't ask what that means." Wesley said. "Please continue. Today I'm just a team member. Let's see if we can find a golden needle in this haystack. Wesley put the box of donuts right in the middle of the group of tables. Go ahead Aaron."

"Okay, this is sort of another brainstorm session."

"What?" It was Ray this time who was surprised. "We've got enough concepts, I'm sure."

"No, we're not going to brainstorm more concepts," Aaron looked at Wesley for reassurance. "We are going to brainstorm concept combinations. We are going to draw lines from left to right connecting possible whole machine concepts. For example, suppose it makes sense to combine A1 with B3, C2, and D5? Using the same color, draw lines or arrows from A1 to B3, then from B3 to C2, then from C2 to D5, and so on."

"I see."

"Some combinations will just make sense and others won't. When we're done, we should have a list of five or ten machines that we can evaluate more carefully. Okay, grab a marker and let's take twenty minutes and find some complete machines. Don't use the same color twice. If we run out of colors, use a dash pattern. Wesley, thanks for the donuts."

Before long, a dozen machine concepts emerged from the flood of sketches, post-it notes, and butcher paper. Like planning a road trip across the United States from the Pacific Ocean to the Atlantic, a red line went from Seattle to Denver to St. Louis to Atlanta and then to Miami. Another line, blue this time, was drawn from Portland to Salt Lake City to Chicago and on to New York. The board was a multicolored map across the continent of concept combinations.

Wesley pulled Aaron aside and suggested that he

assign a team member to prepare a Rating and Ranking chart, a selection matrix to compare all the machine concepts with the customer requirements. Aaron gave the assignment to Ray who stayed late that night and prepared a spreadsheet on his computer. He placed each concept across the top, 'A' through 'L,' and all applicable requirements down the left side of the matrix.

Part 11 – Rate, Rank, and Score

The next day, the team met in the conference room where Ray was prepared to project the matrix on the wall. One of the concepts was chosen as the benchmark or reference machine as a basis of comparison for the rest of the machines. Ray typed a zero in every cell below the reference concept.

Taking one specification requirement or criteria at a time, the team evaluated each of the remaining concepts as being either more favorable (+), same as (0), or less favorable (-), than the reference concept. The debate was lively and sometimes disagreeable which made Aaron flustered. Wesley just smiled and reminded the group that they were just trying to screen out the less suitable concepts and get the selection down to a reasonable level.

Ray summed the columns giving each concept a score, then ranked the concepts based on their relative scores.

"I don't think this is fair." Bryce said leaning back in

his chair with his arms folded. "Some of the criteria is not as important as other criteria and yet we are giving them all the same weight. This is gonna cause some good concepts to fall out of contention for first place."

Aaron looked to Wesley for help.

"You're right Bryce," Wesley said. "This isn't a very comprehensive evaluation, but all we are trying to do is eliminate the very low scoring concepts so we can focus on the rest. We have a couple more exercises to do before we pick the most practical concept."

Bryce remained a little red in the face.

"Aaron, may I suggest the next step?" Wesley asked.

Aaron nodded with relief.

"Without throwing any of the concepts totally out, let's look at the whole group, but focus primarily on the top six or seven ranked machines and brainstorm any combinations of these that we haven't thought of yet. In other words, is there a thirteenth concept that embodies the favorable combination of two or three others?"

The team worked at this for twenty minutes and did indeed identify two more combinations not thought of before. Bryce was instrumental in suggesting a good feature of a lower ranked concept (one of his) that could be added into a new combination with the higher ranked concepts. Concepts 'M' and 'N' were added to the list ranking up there with the good ones.

"Bryce looks a lot happier now," Aaron thought.

To keep the team moving forward, Wesley suggested that they now choose the top five whole machine combinations from the screen matrix and move on to the weighted scoring exercise. The team took a break while Ray prepared the next spreadsheet and Wesley had a coaching session with Aaron.

"Okay." Aaron stood by the wall next to the projection. "As you can see on the wall, we have concepts 'A,' 'C,' 'D,' 'H,' and 'M.' The last one is a combination of 'B' and 'G.' We are now going to score each remaining concept with a weighted-sum. The total score..."

"Hey Aaron." Ray interrupted. "I keep thinking something is missing and I'm wondering if you all agree."

"What is it?"

"Well, all the criteria so far is based on the requirements we got from HTP."

Wesley looked at Ray with interest.

"Well," Aaron asked, "what else is there?"

"Yah," Bryce added. "They are the customer."

"We haven't taken into account schedule and technical risk."

This got everyone in the room thinking.

Ray continued. "Some of these concepts will take longer than the others to design, analyze, build and test. Some of the concepts use existing technology, and some might require doing things that haven't been proven yet."

"What do you suggest Ray?" Wesley said.

"I suggest as a minimum we add a Schedule Risk criteria and a Technical Risk criteria below the customer requirements."

"What about Cost risk?" Kate asked.

"Well, I thought of that but we already have a customer requirement for $30,000 per unit for 10 units, so we can assess cost risk with that requirement."

"Sounds good." Aaron looked around the room for consensus. "Ray, go ahead and add those two criteria. Thanks for bringing that up." We are now going to score each remaining concept with a weighted-sum. The total score for each concept will be the sum of each concepts weighted criteria scores."

Each team member slid their chairs a little closer to the image, while Wesley inched his way to a back corner of the room.

"First," Aaron continued, "we need to weight each requirement or criteria relative to the other criteria in terms of importance. May I suggest each criteria get a weight of 1, 2, 3, 4, or 5..."

"I prefer a percentage." Kate suggested. "That's the way we did it in one of my process improvement classes."

"All right." Aaron said. "How would you propose we use percentages?"

"Well, we give each criteria a number between 0 and 100 percent. The sum of the weight column has to equal 100%."

"That seems kind of a hard way to do it." Bryce said. "We would have to iterate, changing all the numbers over and over again to get them to add up to 100."

"It's okay." Aaron said. "Let's give it a try. Ray, put a

summation function at the bottom of the weight column in the spreadsheet so we can track it. Okay, let's get going. There are 19 criteria; 17 from customer requirements, and the two additional ones we just added. The first Requirement or criteria states, "The AutoBlaster shall remove 100% of the canister material from the flat surface of the cutter." What should the weight be for this one?"

With a little more frustration, the team took a couple hours and finally agreed on weights for each criteria and ratings for each concept. Ray entered equations in the spreadsheet and before long, scores were revealed for the five concepts.

"Okay!" Rey exclaimed. "Concept 'D' is the winner."

"Hm-hmm." Wesley respectfully broke his silence in the corner of the room. "Before we trust the results, we need to trust ourselves and think carefully through the process and the numbers in the spreadsheet. We've had a long day. I suggest we each take a visual image of what's on the wall, sleep on it, and return tomorrow to see if any changes should be made."

Part 12 - Build Prototypes

A week passed since the team decided on their top machine concepts. Aaron had made assignments for each team member to make prototypes of various parts of machines 'D' and 'M' for further discussion and refinement.

Ray worked miracles with cardboard, Styrofoam, wooden dowels and duct tape to show how the cutters would move in and out of the enclosure.

Aaron demonstrated his creative work in plexiglass, nuts, and bolts to show how the diamond cutters would be received and retained into a receptacle containing magnets, then released at the end of the cycle. With a prototype, the team discovered a better way to hold the cutters and release them at the end of the cycle.

Kate searched for potential suppliers of blasting equipment and worked with Ray on the control system diagram consisting of a diagram of boxes and lines with arrows. There were separate boxes for the Controller, main actuator, cutter removing actuator, operator interface, blasting and recovery unit, and actuator sensors. Lines and arrows represented the flow of information, commands and signals, Inputs and Outputs, between the controller and all other elements.

Bryce worked hard on the conceptual Computer Aided Design (CAD) three dimensional model to show how it would all go together.

Aaron worked on the presentation to be given at their first customer design review just around the corner.

Part 13 – Conduct your Design Review

"Where have you guys been!" Aaron complained, arms folded, hands gripping his upper arms as Ray and Bryce entered the conference room. "The Design

Review starts in an hour and I need practice. You were supposed to be here at eight."

"Sorry. We were up in the computer lab working on the cutter sweeper illustration." Bryce handed a thumb drive to Aaron.

"The picture we have in the presentation should be good enough." Aaron said.

"No really," Ray insisted. "I think you'll like this one much better."

Aaron took the thumb drive and plugged it into his laptop sitting on the conference room table. Kate was sitting opposite from Aaron sketching some kind of diagram in her notebook. While Aaron loaded the file and replaced the image in question, he explained that Wesley had already reviewed the presentation and gave a few comments.

"I don't think these guys know how nervous I am," Aaron thought. "I tried to get someone else to be the speaker but..."

"Okay." Aaron adjusted the projector pointed at the whiteboard and called the group to order. "I'm going to try to give this presentation as though it's the real thing. You can stop me if you want, but I'd prefer you wait until the end to make your suggestions."

"Aaron?" Kate leaned back in her chair. "Don't worry. You'll do fine."

"Look who's talking," Aaron thought. "If she were the one giving this presentation, she'd probably be a nervous wreck."

"It's just that there will be many people there,

including our customer, and professors. I even saw some photographers headed toward the presentation rooms."

"Look," Ray said. "We have a great project; nothing to be ashamed of. I think Matt's going to be pleased. Just focus on what we have been doing and everything will be fine. There may be a surprise or two but..."

Kate kicked Ray on the shin under the table.

"What was that all about?" Aaron thought to himself. "Do they know something?"

Aaron stood beside the whiteboard and began. "Welcome. Our sponsor is HTP Diamond and we are team..."

Aaron made it through the dry-run without any difficulty. The team was amazed; he was amazed. A few adjustments were made to the presentation materials and a few suggestions given regarding presentation style. With thirty minutes to spare the team powered down the projector and computer and made their way to the assigned room.

"Did you remember to bring the prototypes?" Aaron asked Ray.

"Yah, they're right here in this box."

Entering the half filled room they greeted Matt Clawson from HTP Diamond and the rest of the HTP team, Jared, Cody, and Peter.

"Aaron." Matt released Aaron's right hand, grabbed his shoulder and turned him in the direction of a distinguished man in a suit, white shirt and tie. "I'd like you to meet Mr. Ben Ericsson. He is the president of HTP Diamond."

"Oh my goodness. Now I'm in trouble." Aaron thought then responded. "How do you do? Thanks... I mean thank you for coming."

"Matt has told me great things about you and your team." Mr. Ericsson said.

"Did he say 'my' team?" Aaron thought.

"And I'm looking forward to seeing your progress." Mr. Ericsson looked for a moment at Jared. "This means a lot to our business, and our employees."

"Talk about pressure," Aaron thought. "Well, if he cares that much about his employees, maybe he won't be so hard on my presentation."

Ray gave Aaron a pat on the back.

Wesley came over and gave Aaron some encouragement then sat with the team on the first row, all dressed in their black polo team shirts with white lettering *AutoBlast*. The HTP employees were seated in the second row.

The Capstone Professor was chairing the design review who, right at the scheduled time welcomed the audience, thanked the sponsors, and introduced the team. Sure enough, the photographer from the university press was standing against the wall adjacent to the first row. The room was now nearly filled with Capstone students and a few others never seen before.

"Hello everyone." Aaron began. "First of all we'd like to thank our sponsor, HTP Diamond who are all seated over here in the second row. We are team AutoBlast."

Each member of the team raised their hand, gave a

little wave, looked back at the audience, then back toward Aaron.

"We have been tasked to develop a system to improve an important process at HTP Diamond. Here is an outline of my presentation."

The photographer clicked a rapid fire of several shots as Aaron pointed at the screen.

"First I will provide a background of HTP Diamond and the current process they..."

Just then someone wearing a leather aviation jacket entered the room that Aaron had not expected.

"I can't believe it," Aaron thought. "I didn't know my dad was coming." Aaron looked over at his team mates who were smiling a little extra.

"I bet Ray told him I was making this presentation," Aaron thought. Aaron noticed a pin on his father's lapel. "It's the World War II fighter. He remembered our conversation."

Wesley cleared his throat.

Realizing he stopped mid sentence, Aaron started again. "After the background, I will show the Customer Needs that we identified, then a sampling of the many concepts we considered, and then a detailed review of our recommended solution and rationale."

Aaron's father sat on the back row, arms folded, with a proud look. Mr. Ericsson sat tall, very attentive, scratching his chin between a thumb and forefinger.

"HTP Diamond makes synthetic diamond cutters used in the oil and gas industry to drill wells." Aaron pointed to the screen at an image of several small metallic objects. "The diamonds are made out of polycrystalline powder sintered at a temperature of 1400 degrees C and about one million psi."

"I wonder why Matt just nudged Mr. Ericsson with his elbow," Aaron thought.

"After the sintering process, the silver-gray canister used to contain the powder must be removed. That's where we come in."

Aaron explained how the process is done now and told the audience of the experience each team member had in September putting on the protective gear and performing the process.

Jared nodded as Aaron demonstrated wiping dust and sweat from his forehead.

Aaron walked the audience through Customer Needs and Requirements, Benchmarking, Concept Generation, and finally Rating and Ranking which led him into several slides of the final recommended machine concept. "Dad is smiling," he observed to himself. "Mr. Ericsson is tapping all his fingers together like a steeple."

The professor in charge notified Aaron that he had five minutes left before his question and answer period.

Aaron pointed at the screen. "The machine will be mounted on a cart so maintenance personnel can move it around, and so it can be used at different sintering cells. The operator places two cutters in the holder at this location then the operator presses two start buttons, for safety. The computer or PLC then commands a three position actuator to move the cutters under the nozzle, one at a time." Aaron pointed to the nozzle mounting position. "When one cutter is blasted, then the actuator moves the cutters to the next position. At the end, the cutters are returned to their loading position where another actuator pushes them off the holder into a container of water. We've prepared a little animation to demonstrate this."

"I hope this video runs okay," Aaron thought.

Aaron pressed a couple buttons on the laptop and ran the video.

"As you can see, this concept should help the operator blast the cutters while having time to perform other duties and while removing him or her from the unhealthy and unsafe environment." Aaron paused until the video completed. "Thank you. Are there any questions."

The professor in charge applauded and the audience followed.

"Okay, Questions?" The professor asked.

"Here we go," Aaron thought. "Take it easy on me."

About five-seconds passed without a hand so the professor said, "What is your greatest concern about the concept you have chosen?"

Aaron was ready for that one. He clicked the remote returning to a prior slide. "SiC blasting is very hostile, not only to the cutters being cleaned, but also to everything inside the blasting chamber. The multi-position actuator must position the cutters in two positions inside the chamber. The holder is held by a precision rod attached to the actuator passing through the bulkhead here." Aaron pointed at the cross-section of the machine on the screen. "We need to design all these parts inside the chamber to withstand the hostile environment for a reasonable amount of time, including the holder, the shaft, and the linear bearings holding the shaft. We anticipate creating a preventative maintenance schedule to have the shaft and other parts replaced periodically by maintenance before they fail."

Aaron turned back around and faced the audience, hands held in front of him, looking back and forth across the group, a little sweat forming on his forehead. Mr. Ericsson raised his hand.

"Oh-oh."

"Yes, Mr...." Aaron cleared his throat. "Mr. Ericsson."

"I wonder if he's worried," Aaron thought.

"Very good presentation Aaron, and a promising design. I'd like to complement the team. If this could be made to work, and work reliably, we will need several of them as soon as possible. How confident are you that you can get it fully designed and tested by the end of the semester?"

Part 14 – Design all the Details

"Hey Bryce, how's the progress on the cart design?" Aaron picked up an aluminum bracket from the table, bent over, squinting at the computer monitor in front of Bryce.

"Well, it's a little frustrating because there are so

many parts involved. I chose to go with the '80/20®' brand for the frame just because the local rep' was willing to do some of the work for me and provided these sample parts."

Aaron sat down at the terminal next to Bryce, typed in his password and picked up a two foot long bar of extruded aluminum, examined the cross-section and the texture, then put it down.

"Actually, all the brands are pretty competitive," Bryce continued, then pointed at the monitor." I should be done with the basic design in a couple days. Have you seen Ray this morning?"

"No, I think he made a trip out to HTP to check on electrical parts."

"What are you working on this morning?" Bryce asked.

"I'm pretty excited about the cutter holder." Aaron selected a folder and model with his mouse then waited for the model to display. "The two cutters will be held in these two cylindrical pockets by magnets under each pocket." Aaron scaled and rotated the image as he pointed to the features. "The operator will place the two cutters into the pockets while being guided by these two half round slots in the shielding material on top. When the process is complete, this shearing block will push both cutters off the magnets into the cooling buckets."

"Won't the cutters tip over and bind on the magnet?"

"No, I don't think so. The bottom edge of the shearing block will be very close to the height of the top of the magnet so it..."

"Good news guys!" Ray called out as he entered the CAD room. I just came from HTP and met the manager of the automation group. I was talking to him about options for the electrical enclosure and guess what? He showed me a machine that would work perfect for us."

"What do you mean?" Aaron and Bryce said in unison.

"They have a machine that they started building a year ago for another project, but they didn't finish it and so the machine is available if we want to use it. It's a frame with a nearly complete control box and a top mounting surface that we can modify and mount our stuff on to. It even has an electronic safety screen installed and all wired up."

"What kind of controller does it have?" Aaron asked.

"What are you talking about?" Bryce protested. "I just spent the last two weeks designing a frame, and now you want me to..."

The computer lab door opened again an in walked Kate clutching her purse in one hand, holding a clear plastic bag in the other. She put the bag of sample cutters on the table and said, "They didn't do it right. I can't believe it. I wrote specific instructions on the nozzle distance, angle, SiC flow rate,... They didn't get all the canister material off the cutters."

"This can't be good," Aaron thought.

"I assume you're talking about the SiC subsystem supplier." Bryce asked. "What was their name?"

"Yes, TurboEtch. Before we commit to them, they need to prove that their blaster and reclaimer will work. I got samples from HTP, wrote procedures, and..."

"Well," Aaron thought, "a couple weeks of smooth sailing, and now a storm. I'd better gather the team and see where we're at."

"I'm sorry to interrupt Kate, but let's all go into the conference room. It's been a week since we coordinated, and we need to check our progress against the schedule anyway."

Part 15 – Collaborate and Solve

Aaron closed the door behind them and noticed that the team's action list hadn't been erased from the whiteboard.

"How convenient," Aaron thought.

It had been three weeks since the design review and customer concept approval, and with major high level decisions behind them, it was essential that they get serious work done on design details.

"I know each of you have major issues you are trying to solve, but let's do it in context of what we decided after the design review." Aaron pointed to the whiteboard and picked up a red dry erase marker. "Let's go through this list one at a time, give status, and state what our problems or risks are. Ray, you go first."

- Multiple Position act. & pneumatics - Ray 50%, Supplier?
- Cutter Holder for two - Aaron 75% Complete, No issues

- Containment Environment - Bryce 10%, Material?
- SiC Blasting and SiC recovery - Kate 25% Repeat test
- Operator Interface w/Start, Stop, etc. - Aaron 10%
- Controller and Software - Kate 25%, S/W License?
- Elect. Cabinet & Components - Ray 50%, Cabinet size?
- Machine Structure, Cabinet, misc - Bryce 50% 0% 75%
- Physical and Electrical Interfaces - Ray No progress
- Documentation (Test procedure, Final Report) Aaron 0%
- CAD Top Assembly - Bryce 25%
- Bill of Materials - Aaron 25%
- Purchasing - Ray 10%
- Schedule - Aaron

"I have found several companies that make pneumatic actuators that will stop at three positions." Ray opened his slim laptop and swiped the mouse pad a couple times. "I've compared three different actuator suppliers and haven't made a decision yet." He pointed at the screen. "I'm leaning toward this one because I've been able to go and see actuators at the local supplier." He turned his computer around for the others to see as he continued. "Here is the model I like best. It meets our movement requirements and should be stiff enough to handle the cantilevered load of the cutter holder, cutters, supporting shaft, and downward blasting force. HTP uses this brand a lot."

"Looks great Ray," Aaron said. "Are you going to order the shearing actuator as well?"

"Yep, as soon as you tell me which one."

"Would you say you are 50% complete on the selection of the actuators?"

"Yeh, that's about right."

"What have you found out about the electrical control cabinet?"

"What a win-fall!" Ray pulled a paper copy of the teams electrical schematic from his computer case and laid it on the table. "I spent the last week looking at enclosures, power supplies, relays, and the typical electrical parts we will need,..."

"That sounds familiar." Bryce said.

"And the cabinet just offered to us by HTP already has most of the components we need. It even has a controller in it."

"Which model?" Kate asked.

"It's a smaller version of the same unit you picked, but there may be enough space to add the I/O expansion module."

Bryce leaned back in his chair, arms crossed, face a little red. "Why didn't they tell us about this machine sooner? I mean, it sounds great but I could've used the last several weeks to work on the blasting enclosure. If we use the existing machine, then I've waisted..."

"Sorry Bryce," Ray said. "Nobody knew about this, and we didn't think to ask if they had a machine we could modify."

"Bryce is a great designer," Aaron thought. "I've got to keep him from getting discouraged."

"Bryce," Aaron said. "You've done a great job on the machine structure. While we sort this out, why don't you give us your thoughts on the blasting enclosure, and any progress you've made. In the mean time Ray, can you get drawings or CAD models for the existing machine from HTP and get them to Bryce so he can check it out?"

"Done!" Ray pointed at his laptop monitor. "They emailed them to me ten minutes ago and I just now posted them on our team server."

Aaron turned to Bryce.

"All right." Bryce said with a puckered smile. "Well, the blasting enclosure needs to adapt to the SiC nozzle, allow penetration for the cutter holder shaft, allow a door for loading and unloading cutters, allow for SiC return to the reclaimer, and it needs to withstand the highly volatile environment without eroding away on the inside. I have a basic concept in work, but it has a ways to go."

"What material are you thinking?" Ray asked.

"Eighth-in steel. It's readily available and we can use the water-jet in the machine shop to cut out the pieces for welding."

"So you've decided to weld it instead of bending it from a cut pattern?" Kate asked. "This kind'a looks like a ventilation duct part, like the register ducts in my house, and most parts like that are bent out of sheet metal."

"I know," Bryce said, "but this needs to be a very heavy gauge and I have a lot of experience welding."

Ray looked up. "I have some welding experience too."

"Do you have any plans," Kate continued, "for treating the inside of the enclosure to prevent SiC from eroding the surface?"

"I thought about it but I don't have any ideas yet. Do you have some?"

"I recall something from a materials class. Let me check one of my textbooks and get back to you."

"That went well," Aaron thought.

"Okay. Thanks Bryce. Thanks Kate." Aaron pointed to the SiC Blasting and Recovery line on the board. "Tell us what's happening with the blasting supplier."

Kate gave an understanding look toward Bryce. "I feel like I've wasted a week or more. I ordered sample cutters from Matt at HTP, sent them to TurboEtch along with clear instructions that they were to record the blasting time and nozzle-to-cutter distance. I asked them to try several different nozzle distances and blast until all the niobium material was gone from the flat surface, recording the amount of time in each case." Kate picked up the bag of cutters, holding them in the palm of her hand. "All they did was blast at one distance, for a fixed amount of time, then they returned the cutters to us for inspection. Most of the cutters still have niobium on them."

Part 16 – Purchase, Fabricate, Assemble

One month passed since the Design Review and, except for a few hick-ups here and there, the team progressed well designing the machine and ordering parts. The machine provided by HTP turned out to be a great help but the electrical control box was too small for all the necessary components. Ray identified and ordered a new larger box and began making preparations to transfer components to the new box. He had to rewire the whole thing. Kate finally got favorable blasting results from TurboEtch and as of yesterday, received approval from HTP to place TurboEtch on contract to build the blasting and re-claiming subsystem. Unfortunately the lead time was four weeks which meant the team would have less than a month to integrate and test the entire unit before the end of the semester, if TurboEtch delivered on time. The good thing was, she could now spend more time focusing on learning how the controller operates and writing the software.

Bryce completed the CAD design of the blasting enclosure, cut all the parts using the onsite water jet, and spent the last few days welding.

"Bryce?" Jay asked as he and Aaron entered the welding booth. "What happened to the enclosure? Why is the flange warped like this?" Jay tipped the enclosure back and forth on two low points on opposite corners. Jay and Aaron noticed that when seated on three corners on a flat surface, the forth corner was raised an eighth of an inch above the surface.

"It warped while welding." Bryce said. "The residual stress in the 3/16 inch thick steel caused bending when it cooled."

"I thought," Ray hesitated. "I thought you specified 1/8 inch steel sheet."

"It was going to take two weeks to get it, so I used

some material they had on hand in the machine shop."

"I hope this doesn't backfire on us," Aaron thought.

"I've already designed and ordered the attachment hardware based on 1/8 inch thickness." Aaron said. "I hope they still fit. Can we reheat the enclosure and get the flange flat?"

"I don't think so, it's pretty stiff. Maybe."

"It's critical," Aaron added, "that the gap between the enclosure and the table be tight so no SiC escapes."

"I know." Bryce said abruptly. "I've been thinking about it all night and maybe I just need to make another one."

"You mean start all over?" Aaron said. "I don't think we have time for that. Can we use a thick rubber gasket to overcome the variance?"

"Let me work on it," Bryce said. "It's thick enough that I may be able to machine it flat on the mill."

"I don't think so," said Ray. "Just heat it up and..."

Kate looked across the room from where she was programming.

Aaron took a deep breath thinking, "These guys are getting heated up."

"Just heat it up and ping it a few times all the way around, just above the flange." Ray insisted. "This should reduce some of the residual stress."

"I don't agree," Bryce said. "That won't look professional. Look, this is my design, let me figure it out."

"Okay." Aaron raised both hands. "Bryce you think it through and let us know what you decide. Ray,"

Aaron pointed across the room to a workbench. "Show me how it's going with the new electrical box. Oh, and by the way, have the actuators come in yet?"

"It looks like I successfully diverted that situation," Aaron thought.

Later in the day Bryce came to Ray and offered to let him try the heating and pinging idea. By the next morning, the team was gathered around the blasting enclosure admiring how well it sat, flat as can be on the mounting surface.

"Thanks Ray," Bryce said. "Not bad."

"Ray!" Kate called out from across the lab. "I can't get this to work. Did you say that you have some PLC experience?"

"Well, a little. But I bet you learned a lot more than I know from your automation class. What's the problem?"

"Wesley helped me lay out the sequence diagram for the machine, but I am having difficulty implementing it."

Ray pointed at a paper on the table. "Is this the diagram?"

"Yes."

Part 17 – Test and Refine

"What's going on?" Bryce said to Ray entering the lab. "Aaron sounded concerned in his voicemail? Why the 7:00 a.m. urgent meeting?"

Ray pointed at the machine. "Look at the test cell.

We are supposed to start testing next week. Does anything look wrong to you?" Bryce scratched his head. "The blasting and reclaiming unit?"

Ray nodded.

"It was supposed to be here yesterday. What happened?"

"Kate got a message from the supplier rep' last night and the unit won't ship until Friday. That means it won't be here until the middle of next week, and it takes time to get it through shipping and receiving..."

Aaron and Kate came into the lab, Aaron's eyes a little red. Kate looked worried.

"Houston," Ray said. "We have a problem."

No one smiled.

"I wish I could laugh," Aaron thought. "I'm glad Ray tries to keep us cheerful."

"Thanks for coming early today." Aaron tossed his notebook three feet over to the table then walked to the machine. We've run into a couple issues." Aaron motioned for everyone to look at the latches on the blasting enclosure. "Last night I installed the new cutter holder, and, while running initial software tests, we found that the enclosure door doesn't open all the way because of an interference."

"I thought," Bryce said, looking at Kate, "that you were gonna tell us about the blasting unit."

"We'll get to that in a minute." Aaron opened the door with his finger as far as it would go, then he moved the cutter holder until it hit the door. "See, the door only opens to about 45 degrees and the cutter holder won't move all the way to the operator loading position."

"Look at the hinge fasteners." Ray said, bending over to look along the hinge axis. "They run into the enclosure flange."

"That's what we noticed," Aaron continued. "It may have something to do with the thickness of the enclosure material because the interference didn't show up on the CAD model."

"Oh no!" Bryce squinted and put his hand on his forehead. "I never changed the CAD model to the 3/16 inch material."

"There might be other reasons," Aaron assured. "I redesigned the cutter holder a few times and I may have increased the height to make room for the magnets without integrating it with the rest of the model."

"Can't we just grind away the flange area where the fasteners hit?" Ray suggested.

"Or," Bryce said, "maybe we could raise the cutter holder and the door and hinge. Then it will have more room to open."

"But if we raise the cutter," Ray countered, "We'll have to raise the supporting shaft, the supporting bearings, and the multi-position actuator. That would affect all the main mounting..."

"Wait you guys," Aaron interrupted. "There is another problem with the cutter holder that I designed, and just yesterday I was thinking I would have to go to the machine shop and make another one. We could relocate the supporting shaft hole a little lower in the cutter holder. This would have the effect of raising the holder without raising the shaft and actuator. This would allow the hinge and door to be raised."

"I'm confused." Kate said. "How is raising the holder going to allow the door two swing further open?"

"Raising the holder," Bryce explained, "allows us to raise the door. Raising the door allows the hinge to pivot further without hitting the fasteners on the enclosure flange."

"Oh, I see it now. Then I agree with Ray. Don't go to all that work. Besides, it may cause other problems we can't see yet. Just shorten the fasteners or grind slots in the flange. This is just a prototype anyway."

"You're right Kate." Aaron said. "I wanted it to be perfect for HTP, but we've run out of time and we can make recommendations for them to improve it later. What's most important is that we deliver a reliable working prototype."

"I worked so hard," Bryce said, "making the enclosure look good... Now you want to grind slots in it?"

Everyone was quiet.

"I see," Bryce continued, "that this is the best way."

"You're a good sport Bryce." Aaron assured.

"And a very good welder." Ray added.

"I'll get the grinder ready over in the welding booth." Bryce headed for the other end of the lab. "Will you guys mark the interference points, then disassemble the enclosure and bring it over?"

"Weren't we going to talk about the blasting unit?"

Kate looked at Aaron.

"Let's let Bryce get ready." Aaron said. "We can talk about the blaster while we disassemble the enclosure."

While they worked, the team adjusted the schedule, re-planing the testing time for later next week leaving only a few days for testing.

"Kate," Ray suggested, "I've been thinking. We don't need the blasting unit to run your software, at least the part that commands the multi-position and shearing actuators, and monitors all the sensors."

"This may save us," Aaron thought. "Good thinking Ray."

"True," Kate replied. "I can disable the blaster sensor and run the software, making the controller believe the blaster is operating. We should be able to test all the other functions, the start buttons, the actuator movement, the timing, the safety screen,... Yes, I'll make those adjustments and we can still get started with that part of the testing as early as tomorrow. Aaron, is the test procedure ready."

"Yes, I'll print a copy so you can check off each step as you go. You guys are awesome." Aaron said raising both hands in the air.

Bryce looked over from the welding booth.

"You too Bryce, you're all awesome."

Bryce notched the enclosure flange and had it reassembled an hour later. Aaron decided against remaking the cutter holder now that the door opened properly. Testing continued the next day with numerous adjustments to the software, and the procedures. When the blasting unit finally arrived, a couple days were needed to unpack, set it up, connect electrical and ventilation, and connect it to the machine.

Nearly all the assembly and test time was consumed leaving only a couple days for testing before the promised delivery date.

"Matt?" Aaron spoke into his cell phone.

"Yes Aaron," Matt Clawson said. "Did everything get assembled and tested as planned?"

"Well, it's assembled, but due to a few issues, all we've been able to do is power it up a couple times. The blasting unit just got here a few days ago so we did most of our machine testing, you know, moving the cutter holder in and out, without the blaster and reclaimer. We feel pretty good about the software, the electrical, and all the supporting equipment."

The phone was silent for a few seconds.

"I'll tell you what," Matt said. "Instead of testing the unit twice, once at the university and once here at HTP, we have some space right now in our testing area. Let's move the whole system over here and do all the testing. That way our maintenance crew and operators will be able to get familiar with the equipment while you finish your testing."

"That would be great." Aaron said. "Are you sure you have the utilities we need in your testing area like sufficient compressed air, flow rate, power, and ventilation?"

"Yah, I'm pretty sure, but I'll go check on it today.

You send me the facility requirements, and I'll get it ready."

Part 18 - Deliver, Install, Demonstrate

A week passed and the unit was up and running at HTP Diamond. A nozzle was lost in transit, but the supplier was able to get a new one quickly. Also, the pneumatic pipes in the HTP Lab had to be enlarged in order to get enough flow for the blaster. A few days beyond the original planned demonstration date, the team powered up the machine and successfully loaded and cleaned two cutters. They ran a few cycles and then turned it over to Jared, the HTP operator.

"I've been looking forward to this for months." Jared said, putting on his head gear.

Peter, the safety engineer was on hand to verify that the safety screen would prevent hazards to the operator. "I've been recording the sound level during the last two demonstrations." He put his hand on Jared's shoulder. "You won't need the extra hearing protection."

Jared smiled.

Bryce smiled.

"Okay." Kate said to Jared. "Put a cutter in each pocket on the cutter holder, then press both start buttons simultaneously, then back away."

Jared placed a cutter part-way into one of the pockets. The magnet snapped the cutter into position. Jared repeated with another cutter, pulled his hands away from the enclosure, and pressed down on both buttons. The fan on the blasting reclaimer came on while the cutter holder disappeared into the blasting enclosure. The enclosure door snapped shut sealing the chamber. A muffled hissing sound emanated from inside. After about 15 seconds the hissing stopped and the actuator clicked to the second position. The hissing resumed another 15 seconds then stopped. The enclosure door popped open and the cutter holder returned to the load position displaying two clean cutters, niobium free. The shearing actuator pushed both cutters from the holder into the two cooling cups.

"Oh yeh!" Jared exclaimed. "Get me some more cutters."

There were 'high-fives' all around the test cell as other employees looked toward the excitement at the new machine with wonder. Wesley stood behind the team with a proud look. Matt looked down the hall and saw Mr. Ericsson looking through the lab window. Matt made a fist with his thumb pointing up.

Aaron felt like he had just set foot on the moon thinking to himself, "It was hard, but it was worth it. I wish my dad was here."

Mentor Discussion and Exercises

Aaron, Ray, Kate, and Bryce are typical of many engineering teams, sometimes working independently, sometimes working together, always working to a common goal of meeting the customers requirements.

In Cutting Edge we get a sense for how important favorable results might be to our customer, how customer needs are obtained and requirements developed and then used to evaluate the solution, how benchmarking, brainstorming and concept generation are critical to obtaining a good solution.

1. How did this team react, individually and as a whole, to setbacks and problems?
2. Would you say that Aaron was a good leader?
3. How would you have led the team through each crises?
4. What role did the coach play?
5. Should the most experience person make all the decisions?

Product Development is a great adventure creating new or improved solutions, combining creative and academic skills, managing and nurturing relationships to bring the best out in everyone involved.

6. What engineering skills were necessary for this project?
7. What resources did team members use to find options and answers?
8. Where did they go to get inspiration?
9. What did they do when there was disagreement?
10. What did this team do well?
11. What could this team have done differently to be more successful?

6 - SPEED READER

Richard held a take-out box on his lap. "Thanks for driving. Beef Broccoli was just what I needed."

"Oh yah." Eric answered taking a quick look over his right shoulder at the foam box on the back seat. "And you can't go wrong with Cashew Chicken."

"I'm so glad the test is over." Richard continued. "Now I can summarize the data and get back to a few other projects that've been on hold."

Eric stopped his car at an intersection. "I'd say it went pretty smooth, considering all that safety and regulatory stuff you were required to satisfy."

"Uh-huh, but the worst part was having all those people in the lab, looking over my shoulder, pencils in hand, ready for any failure. I'm tired."

Eric asked, "Why didn't they give you more time?"

"I guess they're waiting for it in the field. They absolutely had to have it done and shipped today. Besides, the truck is on its way." Richard pulled two theater tickets from his shirt pocket and tapped them on his knee. "I'm gonna finish the report, clean my desk, and get ready for Monday"

"What movie you and Kathy going to tonight?"

"Oh, its not a movie. We have tickets to a play, 'My Fair Lady.'"

As Richard and Eric pulled into the parking lot, David, their manager walked toward the car, arms stretched out to his side, palms up, mouth open.

"Uh-oh." Eric looked at Richard. "Since when does Dave come out to greet us after lunch? Did he want to go with us?"

"We need you guys right now out at the test bay," David said before Richard and Eric shut their doors. "Kevin, the customer Quality Representative is concerned about the brake on the hoist and doesn't think our testing was sufficient."

Caught off guard, Richards grip compressed the Styrofoam box in his hand. "Why," he thought, "would he wait until the last minute to criticize my work, especially after all the revisions I made for him?"

Richard spoke, "Why is he worried about--"

Eric jumped in. "Why didn't he say something

yesterday? They've had the procedure for weeks."

Richard tried again. "What caused this concern for the brake. I double-checked the specification..." Richard caught himself and looked at Eric, "We checked the specifications thoroughly and the hoist meets the holding load requirements."

David walked briskly up the hill motioning his two engineers to follow. "They are concerned that if the brake doesn't completely stop and hold when the motor is off, that the load could drop without warning and cause damage or hurt someone."

"The supplier assured us," Richard said, "that the brake can take three-times the load when the power is off."

"Regardless, they are insisting on another test." David pointed to a semi-truck parked on the side of the road. "And it has to be done today."

Richard and Eric followed David toward the building they had lived in for the past five days.

"OK." Richard took a deep breath and turned to Eric. "It shouldn't be too hard to repeat a couple paragraphs in the procedure. Is the instrumentation still hooked up?"

"Uh-huh."

David held the door as the three made their way into the test bay finding most of the visitors still present, some examining documents, others inspecting the hoist still installed on the overhead rails above the test pit. As Richards eyes settled into the test pit, the Beef Broccoli settled in the pit of his stomach, unpleasantly lubricated by the smell of hydraulic oil, and the light sweat on his face. Putting on his best behavior, for a Friday afternoon, Richard glanced at Eric suggesting he do the same, then turned to the group.

"I understand you would like to repeat some tests."

"Well, not exactly," Kevin said. "I don't think repeating tests will prove the capability of the brake."

"What is your concern with the brake?"

"Uh, we aren't sure that the brake will hold the load stationary when the power is turned off, or even when the power is on and the operator commands it to stop. One of the inspectors thought they saw the hoist slip when it was holding the test load in the upper position."

"Can you remember which test we were on when it happened?"

"No, but his observation is enough to give me concern and I can't in good conscience sign-off on the test."

Richard stood with his eyes slightly squinted, thumb and index finger rubbing his chin, listening and thinking at the same time. "There's got to be a quick solution. I could show him the safety margin in the supplier specification, but he will not accept that."

"The only way," Richard said, "to confirm that the hoist is perfectly locked in the power off state, or in any state, is to monitor motor shaft movement, and there is no provision on this motor to do that."

David looked from Richard's face to Kevin's, but Kevin stood resolute.

Richard put his take-out box on the workbench,

grabbed a tape-measure, took a quick measurement on the hoist motor, then moved toward the whiteboard hanging on the wall. "Gather round everyone. Let's get our heads together 'n' figure this out." Richard erased the testing schedule, several calculations, and a pattern of Xs and Os, someones depiction of a botched football play.

"Now," Richard began, "the typical way to monitor motor speed is with an encoder mounted to the shaft. Since this motor doesn't have one, we need to determine another method for measuring shaft speed." Richard drew a circle in the middle of the whiteboard around the two words, *Shaft Speed*. He then drew a couple radial spokes arching outward from the circle. "OK, how can we measure shaft speed? Give me some practical, and some creative options."

Kevin, having raised a cloud over the day raised his pencil and said, "We could paint a white dot on the end of the shaft a little off center and capture the movement with a video camera."

"That won't work," Eric said. "The shaft is too small and you can't see a few degrees of rotation just by looking at a spot on the shaft. Besides, we don't have any time-tagging video equipment to synchronize the movement."

Richard wrote on the board and waited for Eric to finish. "Let's write the idea down, even though it may seem to have some limitations. It may lead us to something that will work."

David, stood with one hand overlapping the other, tapping on his watch. "What would it take to buy an encoder this afternoon? Let's just install an encoder and rerun the necessary tests."

Again Eric replied, "I've tried before, there's no place local to get an encoder. Perhaps if we found just the right encoder on another motor..."

David's eyes opened wide. "I'll go right now and look in storage. Maybe there's a motor with an encoder that could be removed."

Richard and Eric looked at each other surprised obviously reading each other's minds.

Richard thought, "Since when did David help us find parts. This must really be important to him."

Although doubtful, Richard wrote the idea on the board. Holding up the tape measure he said, "The shaft extends out of the motor body only one-eighth of an inch, so it doesn't appear that we can clamp anything to it."

From a step ladder near the hoist, a customer representative said, "I notice there's a hole in the end of the shaft. Perhaps we can thread the hole and bolt an extended shaft on the end?"

The proof test cell technician added, "Or even use it to attach something else."

"I'm sorry," Kevin shook his head, "we can't permanently modify the deliverable hardware. Technically, such a modification would require a rerun of all the tests."

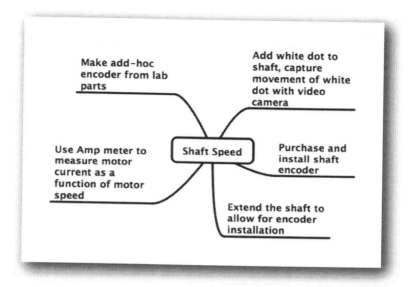

The technician put one eye close to the shaft. "But I think it's already threaded."

Richard added all the ideas to the board. "Is there any way to measure motor speed without connecting or doing something to the shaft?"

Eric reached around and scratched the back of his head. "Well, the speed of a motor is related to the electrical current. We could use an amp meter to capture the current, then calibrate the speed as a function of current."

Most heads in the room nodded up and down.

Eric paused. "Oops, we still need a definitive way to measure speed to calibrate the measurement, to correlate it with current."

Getting discouraged, Richard added the Amp meter to the list, but remained hopeful that one of these options could be made to work. He discretely took a look at his watch. "Its time for a change in perspective. Eric, let's go over to the old lab and see if we can get inspired. The rest of you, please keep thinking."

Richard and Eric discussed the options as they walked.

"I'm gonna miss the play tonight, aren't I?" Richards head hung down. "How am I gonna tell Kathy?" Richards mind wandered back to the ticket booth at the theater where he walked through a rotating 'turn-style' to get the tickets.

He thought, "There was a digital counter that incremented each time a person passed through the turn-style."

"What we need is something that could be attached to the shaft without damaging it," Richard said, "and then have that something trigger a signal as the shaft rotates, preferably multiple counts per rotation."

"You mean create our own encoder?"

"Yes." Richard pressed for fundamentals. "What are the basic elements of an encoder?"

"Well, most of them contain some kind of optical disc with radial patterns or slits..." Eric's eyebrow raised. "Actually, an encoder is like a bar-code except the black and white patterns are not in lines, they're in concentric circles around the disc. The disc rotates near a small sensor array or scanner that reads the nearest pattern on the disc. With enough circles and patterns they can give a very accurate reading of the shafts angle, like on the order of arc-seconds. They come in absolute and relative--"

"No, no. Thats too much accuracy for what we need? Is there a low-end encoder, something that just tells us a dozen or a hundred readings each time the shaft rotates?"

"Well, there's an opto-coupler--"

"An opto what?"

"A slotted opto-coupler. It's a little U-shaped device, like a tiny goal-post." Eric held both arms up in the air. "Imagine a light on one post, and a light sensor on the other. When the football passes between the light and the sensor, the sensor is triggered."

Richard gave a funny grin.

"Look," Eric continued, "you know the conveyor at the grocery story checkout where you put your food to pay for it. The conveyor belt moves the food toward the checker and when the food gets to the end of the belt, the belt stops. It stops because on one side of the belt is a light, and on--"

"Ya, ya I get the idea." Richard said. "The same principle is used on all kinds of conveyor belts to detect objects or to count them. So, we just need a light source, like an LED (Light-emitting-diode), and a light sensitive switch, like a photodiode, and we have our own opto-coupler."

"Slotted opto-coupler," Eric corrected. "That's basically it. We provide a power supply, a measuring device to capture the signal, and--"

"Hey guys!" David called from across the way. "No

motors with encoders in supply."

"We're headed to the lab to look for parts or options. Can you go take care of our guests in the test cell?" Richard turned back to Eric. "OK, is there something common in the lab that is similar to what we need? Where can we find... can we make our own LED-photodiode pair out of individual components? Can we make our own disc?"

In the back of the lab, Richard and Eric made their way between two rows of cabinets filled and covered with leftovers from years of testing. Like a surplus store for electronics, they looked over oscilloscopes, multi-meters, drawers of resisters and capacitors, rolls of wire, power supplies. Eric paused by some old printers and typewriters, dragging two fingers through the dust on the printer paper tray. He picked up a shiny round object covered with letters, about the size of a golf ball, and rolled it between his fingers. "Wow, this is cool. I've heard about these." He rolled it some more letting the alphabet press into his skin then looked close as the character marks faded.

Sliding a bulky dot-matrix print head back and forth across the guide rails of an old printer Richard asked, "How does the printer motor, or controller know to stop when the print head reaches the end of travel?"

After closer examination, they observed a small flange, a little flat piece of metal or plastic attached to the print carriage. When pushed to the end of travel, the flange passed between the two sides of a black U-shaped...

"Look, an opto-coupler!" they both called out simultaneously.

"The tab breaks the light path in the coupler," Richard surmised.

"Sending a signal to the controller," Eric said.

"Do you think this straight line mechanism could be modified into a 'rotary' device? We could mount a tab, a long thin piece of metal to the motor shaft. If the opto-coupler were mounted on the motor body so that the tab passes through it each revolution, then we would have our encoder."

"Not quite," Eric cautioned. "We need multiple pulses or indications per revolution in order to prove the shaft isn't turning. With just one tab, the shaft could slip or rotate slowly within one turn and we wouldn't know it until it moved far enough for the flange to pass through the opto-coupler again."

"Then we need multiple flanges. Here look." Richard opened his lab book and carefully drew a disc with several radial slots and a hole in the middle. "Let's have the machine shop make a disc that can be mounted to the end of the shaft."

"Excellent," Eric said. "And how will we attached the opto-coupler to the motor, duct tape?"

With screw driver and wire cutters, Richard and Eric removed the opto-coupler from the old printer and headed for the exit hoping that the machine shop would squeeze this important project into their busy schedule.

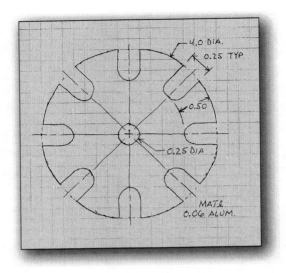

"Can you believe it?" Richard said as he examined the coupler in his hand. "Finding just what we needed on an old printer."

"You want it when?" the machine shop supervisor said. "You guys know the shop closes at three on Fridays, and we still have jobs to finish."

Richard looked at his watch.

"But this is hot," Eric said. "We've got a delivery, a test that has to be done today. See that truck across the street?"

"Sorry guys, everyones job is hot, and two of my technicians have already gone home."

Eric moved closer to the supervisor. "Would you at least look at the sketch and tell us if it could be done quickly?"

While Eric leaned on the supervisor, Richard stared

at the sketch, thinking, "Wait a minute. This looks like something I've seen before. What was it? Where was it?" He looked around the machine shop, and the adjoining office. "The printer? No, there's nothing in an ink jet that looks like a disc." Then his mind wandered back to the lab, again walking down the rows of parts and old machines. He saw in his mind the dot matrix printer, and next to it an old typewriter, with... "Hey! Daisywheels!"

The supervisor lifted both eyebrows. Eric turned.

"Eric, those daisywheels look almost just like this sketch."

"What daisywheels?"

Richard headed for the door. "I'll be right back."

Grabbing a couple of wheels he examined them closely, thinking, "It might be possible to mount one on the motor shaft. Not only is the diameter about right, but the daisywheel spokes are numerous and equally spaced."

Richard continued to talk to himself oblivious to anyone else in the room. Laying one of the wheels down, he clamped the other between his fingers then fanned a few spokes with his other hand. "Daisywheel spokes traveling through the opto-coupler would give us a continuous pulse vs. speed indication. We can count the total number of spokes, therefore we would know the number of pulses per revolution, and we could have our encoder within the hour."

Richard ran back to the machine shop holding up

the daisywheel with pride. "Look. This will be perfect. It already has the hole in the middle. We can mount the daisywheel to the motor shaft, mount the opto-coupler to the motor body, you can run the wiring to the instrumentation, and away we go."

Richard and Eric grabbed a few bolts and washers of different diameters to mount the wheel and off they ran to the test cell.

Thirty minutes later, after installing the hardware, writing a few more steps of procedure, and getting approvals from everyone, their test began. The strip-chart recorder (yes, a strip-chart recorder) spit out paper with pulses collectively representing motor speed consistently and clean.

"Now we will know exactly when the shaft is turning," Richard said.

"And when it is not!" Eric said a little louder than necessary.

A large group hovered over the recorder while the technician used the pendant to command the hoist up and down.

"Awesome," Eric said. "Look at these beautiful pulses." Eric's index finger moved back and forth as the paper rolled out of the machine. "And look." Eric motioned to the technician. When you commanded the hoist to stop, the pulses immediately stopped." Eric looked at Kevin, "And stayed stopped."

After a few test runs and another roll of strip chart paper, the conclusive start and stop tests where completed. Richard felt great, Eric was beaming, David was relieved, Kevin was satisfied, and the hoist was prepared for shipment (without the add-hoc encoder and duct tape).

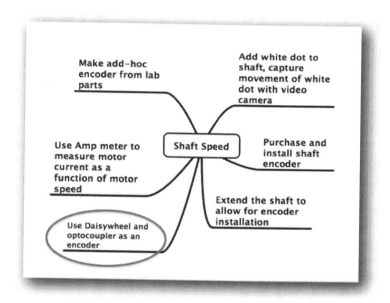

"Richard, way to go." Eric held his hand in the air and Richard matched with a high-five. "I'm so glad you remembered those daisywheels."

"Hey, look what happens when you go looking through antiques."

"I'll never forget the look on the shop supervisors face," Eric said with a chuckle, "when you burst into the machine shop holding up a daisywheel, the solution to our problem."

Richard took a deep breath, picked up his cold take-out box, leaned against a workbench, and stared at the whiteboard. "That's what I like about engineering, " he thought, "diving into problems with determination, keeping your head, then epiphany; those amazing moments of sudden revelation, or insight. Nothing could compare to it, not even leftover... Beef Broccoli."

Later that evening, as Richard and Kathy enjoyed the play, each time Eliza Doolittle stepped in front of a potential customer holding up a flower, all Richard could see was the look on Eric's face (and the supervisor), when he burst through the shop door, holding up his daisywheel.

As the show progressed, Richard's adventure that day increased his appreciation for the experiences of others. Kathy turned to see Richard intently listening as Professor Higgins inspired his literary challenged student to accomplish a task well worth the pursuit. "Think what you're dealing with [Eliza]. The majesty and grandeur of the English language, it's the greatest possession we have. The noblest thoughts that ever flowed through the hearts of men are contained in its extraordinary, imaginative, and musical mixtures of sounds. And that's what you've set yourself out to conquer Eliza. And conquer it you will."

"Engineering is like a noble composition," Richard thought. "It is extraordinary, imaginative, and like a musical mixture of sounds.

Mentor Discussion and Exercises

Have you ever completed a project, or thought you completed a project just to find out that there was more that needed to be done, right at the last moment? After working hard on this project Richard and Eric were looking forward to moving on. Who do you relate to in this story? Richard, Eric, David, Kevin? Or perhaps Kathy? As a manager, David was feeling pressure to get the project completed and delivered on time. Kevin felt responsibility for making sure the product would be safe under all conditions. Eric felt insulted that Kevin would voice his concern so late in the game. And Richard was worried about his date that night with Kathy.

1. Did anyone do anything wrong in this story, or was it just unfortunate timing and circumstance?

Engineering projects like this are usually done by a detailed and well written specification and at the end of the project, before the product is delivered, a detailed and well written test procedure is prepare, reviewed, adjusted, and agreed upon by all the necessary parties. Eric had a good point about the procedure being previously approved, but in the spirit of safety and a happy customer, it just might be best to go the extra mile.

2. What method did Richard use to develop possible solution ideas?

3. Who did he involve in the brainstorm?
4. Did the final solution exist in the test lab?
5. Where did Richard and Eric go to get more ideas?

Often, we can shift our thinking by examining other products or processes that do different things but have similar processes to our need.

6. How could an old technology printer provide a solution to a later technology problem?

In this case, a simple opto-coupler would satisfy the need. There just might be an opto-coupler near you; in a printer or scanner, in a DVD player, in some other electronic device with moving parts.

7. What other methods could be used to capture or measure motor shaft speed, other than an optical encoder?
8. How well did Richard handle the pressure?
9. Did he show respect for everyone else?
10. What would have happened if he lost his temper, refusing to risk his date with Kathy that evening?

Showing respect and understanding for the opinions and needs of your team mates and customers is very powerful in maintaining and building relationships and in finding the best solutions. In fact, when you show integrity and respect, others will trust and respect you, opening the way for favorable options in your career. In addition, by keeping their heads, Richard and Eric found satisfaction in creative and simple solutions.

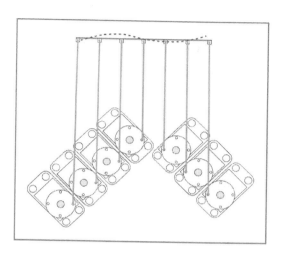

7 - THE RIBBON CUTTING

"That's impossible! It can't be done."

Trying to strum a few relaxing chords on his guitar late one evening, Kevin recounted over and over Jack's words earlier that day at work. "There's no way you're going to get seven precision motors packed into such a small space!"

Kevin's engineering log book was open on the floor slightly overlapping his favorite music book. He tried to focus on the song, but kept clutching his instrument with both arms, heavily distracted by the challenge of designing a computer-controlled flexible cutter for a new machine at work.

"Maybe he's right." Kevin thought. "Or is Jack just trying to protect his baby, his machine?"

Kevin and Jack were engineers at Banner Label. Banner specialized in producing high quantity adhesive-backed labels on large rolls sold to scrapbook suppliers. Following printing, each roll of labels was installed on a reel-to-reel die cutting machine that cut just deep enough to sever the label face but not the backing. The unique thing about Banner cutters was that they seldom cut straight lines, like the kind used on a sheet of self-adhesive address labels. Banner was known for printing labels with curved graphics and curved edges around the perimeter. For example, the roll of test labels Kevin and Jack were using on their prototype machine had images of curved or wavy ribbons, each individual label being a flat image of a ribbon waving in the breeze. Instead of a straight cut between each label, Banner tried to match the cut to the outermost shape of the graphic.

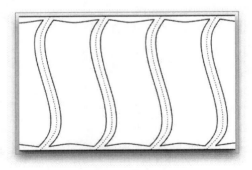

Kevin pulled a small black object from his pocket and laid it on the floor. "There has got to be a way to mount these one-inch wide motors close enough to each other to control push-rods that are only three-quarters of an inch apart. But how?"

"Kevin," He remembered the conversation with his manager the week before. "I'm assigning you to work with Jack in taking the prototype cutting machine to the next level. You need to figure out a way to control the shape of the blade automatically from batch to batch or from roll to roll."

Jack designed and built the reel-to-reel machine but it was Kevin's responsibility to design and build the automated cutter.

Within a couple days Kevin developed the basic concept. A thin steel blade about an inch wide, twenty-thousandths thick, and about four and a half inches long. Bonded to one flat side of the blade were seven pivot blocks for pushing and pulling on the blade. Kevin temporarily installed push rods to each pivot block and then provided a way to clamp the push rods so the cutting blade could be manually shaped and held in place during a test run. As the labels passed under the cutter, the sharpened blade was hit from above, causing it to move a few thousandths of an inch downward, cutting the label face.

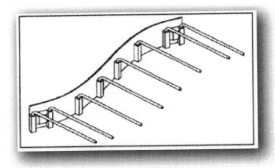

For the next three days Kevin struggled with the requirement to actuate and control the small rods. He filled page after page of sketches in his notebook. Some ideas used mechanical links, some included little pneumatic (air) pistons; he even drew an array of bicycle brake or shift cables, one for each rod, to fan-out the actuated end from the controlled end. Occasionally he would go back and review the fundamental requirement to see if he missed something.

"The plan is to push the seven control rods with servomotors controlled by a PC computer, thereby achieving the desired shape of the blade."

Kevin gripped his guitar pick more firmly than usual. "If we can do this, it will be a great accomplishment. It will reduce downtime. We won't have to change the blade between batches. The operators can remove and replace label rolls, enter a new batch number into the computer, and cut the next batch with only a minute or two of downtime."

He looked out the window for a moment. "Besides, it would be great to prove Jack wrong."

He looked through his sketches again.

"The control rods are three-quarters of an inch apart," he thought. "The servomotors are one inch wide, too large to fit side-by-side to drive the control rods."

He threw his pencil down on his notebook creating a lead divot in the page.

"There is no way," he thought, "without a lot of cables or something, to mount seven large motors closely together to drive rods that are three-quarters of an inch apart."

"My B-string sounds flat." With his left hand Kevin reached under and around the guitar neck and held the third string against the fretboard between the third and fourth frets. He repeatedly plucked the second and third strings, paused to adjust the center tuning peg on the far side of the headstock, then returned to pluck the strings again.

"Whoa!" Kevin stopped plucking and rotated the guitar for a close view of the headstock. "Look at that," he said out loud.

"There are six strings on... oh, I'd say about three-eighths inch spacing, and they are being controlled by actuators that are separated by about an inch. The actuators are bigger than the spacing. That's exactly what I need."

Kevin reached over the guitar and grabbed his engineering notepad and sketched...

"Darn, the led's broken."

He found another pencil and sketched the fretboard

and headstock including the six strings and tuning pegs.

"All I have to do is offset the servomotors at different distances from the cutter, like these tuning pegs, and I should be able to control seven push rods that are only three quarters of an inch apart."

Kevin put his guitar quickly but carefully aside, and drew a sketch of the flexible die-cutter showing servomotors spread out at an angle moving away from the blade.

Kevin smiled and thought, "Why didn't I see this before? There are a lot of instruments like this. The piano, and my mom's autoharp have strings stretching out to different lengths. Who would have thought I'd find a solution in a musical instrument. "

Kevin took a deep breath. "There are solutions to engineering problems everywhere."

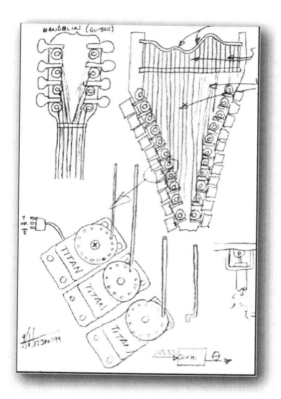

(The next day)

"Jack!" Kevin called out before he could see if Jack was in his cubicle."

"Slow down. What are you so excited about, Kevin?" Jack sat back in his chair, hands clasped behind his head.

"I was playing my guitar last night and, ... well anyway, I know how to drive closely packed rods with a string of motors." Kevin plopped his engineering pad down on Jack's desk.

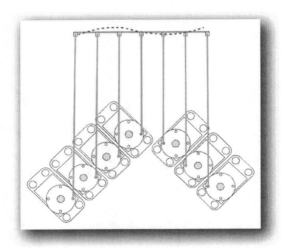

Jack leaned forward slowly and examined Kevin's sketch. "What happened here."

"Oh I dropped my pencil..."

"It looks like you were playing darts with your pencil."

Kevin pointed to the sketch.

"Yes, I see... Yah this might work." Jack acknowledged. "We may have to restrain the side-to-side motion of the rods so the longer ones don't buckle, but that shouldn't be a problem." Jack dropped his shoulders. "Way to go, Mr. Guitar Man."

Kevin lingered in Jack's cube, hands on hips, taking in the moment a little longer.

"Now that you know how to mount the motors

relative to the cutter," Jack interrupted Kevin's delight, "how are you going to determine the commanded position of each motor to achieve the required shape?"

Kevin squinted both eyes. "What are you talking about?"

"Well," Jack picked up a copy of the label they were using to test the prototype machine.

"Look at the shape of the ribbon." Jack moved his pencil slowly along the long wavy edge of the ribbon. "When controlling the servomotors, have you figured out to what position each motor should be driven to create this shape?"

Kevin scratched the top of his head. "Not yet. But I should be able to fit a mathematical curve along the ribbon edge and then move along that curve to find the position for each pivot block."

"I'm not sure it's that straight forward. Sounds like another good engineering challenge," Jack said, "and a math problem as well."

"I'll lay out the servomotor support structure and mounting provisions today." Kevin picked up his book and left Jack's cube. "I'll get going on the curve fitting problem tomorrow."

"By the way," Jack called out over the wall, "have you figured out how you are going to electrically connect and control the servomotors with the computer?"

"Not yet," Kevin called back, "but I plan to get options from Janet, our resident double-E (electrical engineer) in a day or two."

Kevin spent the rest of the day designing a mounting plate for the seven servomotors fanned out in a V shape just like on his guitar. For the prototype, Kevin chose large hobby servos used in remote controlled model airplanes. They were very inexpensive and easy to acquire. Each servo had a disc on the output that rotated to a precise angular position. He designed control rods to attach to the servo disc on one end, and to the cutter blade pivot blocks on the other end.

Kevin asked one of the engineering CAD (Computer Aided Design or Drafting) designers to complete the design so the servomotors and cutter assembly would fit over the top of the label cutting board.

"Now, what shall I work on next?" Kevin thought. "I have to figure out the electrical interface between the controller and the servomotors. I also have to develop the math and write the software to drive the servomotor to positions that will shape the cutter as close as possible to the desired shape. I'd better figure out the electrical interface first in case we need to purchase something. I can work on the math and software while the items are on order."

"Janet." Kevin found Janet out in the loud printing area looking into a machine control box while holding a schematic. "I need some ideas on how to interface and control a large number of small servomotors."

"Kevin," Janet removed an ear plug from one ear. "Will you hold this schematic for a minute while I..."

Janet reached into the cabinet with a small screw driver. "Kevin, stand back a little. You're blocking the light."

"Oh, sorry."

She adjusted a small device on a circuit board while watching a voltmeter that was teetering on top of the cabinet. "There. That should do it. I don't know why the maintenance technician couldn't fix this last night. The instructions are right here in the maintenance manual."

Janet closed the control box and retrieved the schematic from Kevin. "Okay. Now what were you saying about servomotors?"

Kevin pulled a servomotor from his pocket.

"That's the smallest motor I've seen around here," Janet said.

"Actually, it's one of the largest hobby motors available for remote controlled airplanes, boats, or cars. It's a pulse-width-modulated (PWM) device and..."

"Yes, I know." Janet interrupted. "I have a model airplane. Many servo systems use that control technique. There are three wires going to the motor. One is a DC voltage source, one is electrical ground, and the other is the PWM signal operating at 50 hertz."

"As I understand it," Kevin said, "the signal is a DC square wave. The controller, or receiver in the case of an airplane, sends a square wave to the motor at a relatively constant frequency while varying the pulse width depending on the desired servomotor angular output."

"Thats right." Janet confirmed squinting one eye.

"You're pretty smart for a mechanical engineer. These servomotors have a variable resister or potentiometer inside mounted to the output shaft to measure the angle. There is also an onboard integrated circuit chip that compares the desired angle with the actual angle. If there is an error, the chip increases or decreases the pulse width to the motor to drive it in the direction needed to reduce the error to zero. It's a first-order servo."

Kevin hadn't heard that term in a while.

"That means the commanded speed is proportional to the error."

"I remember. The greater the error, the greater the speed." Kevin repeated. "So, how do I generate a pulse-width-modulated square wave in a PC? How do I control these servomotors from the computer?"

"Well," Janet said, "what options have you considered? Have you looked online for plug-in PC circuit boards that will do this?"

"Not yet. I thought maybe you could save me a little time."

"Why did you decide to use a hobby servo? Why don't you go to a larger servo like these?" Janet pointed at some large motors on a press machine as they walked. These companies make motors and controllers that are already tuned to work together."

"No. I can't use big motors like that." Kevin opened his notebook and laid it on a closed toolbox. "Look, I need to individually drive seven rods that are really close to each other. Besides, I don't need that much force or torque."

Kevin laid the hobby servo on top of the sketch aligned with one of the motors drawn on the page.

Janet stood silent, looking at the drawing. She looked up and across the factory at a printing machine some distance away. Then she looked back down at the paper.

"Come with me." Janet walked toward a machine. "I wonder what kind of device the designers used to increase or decrease the flashing speed of the status light on that machine?"

"What did you say?" Kevin said as they got closer to the machine.

Janet looked at the control panel then yelled. "That's it! You could use a counter-timer chip."

"Please explain." Kevin cupped his hands behind his ears.

"See this switch? When you put it in the *Standby* position, the light tower on the top flashes slowly. But when the machine is running it flashes faster. I bet they used a counter-timer chip. Let's go to my desk and I'll show you," Janet said removing the ear plug from her other ear.

Janet sat at her desk and typed "counter timer integrated circuit" into her search engine. "Here it is. 9513!"

"What's a 9513?" Kevin asked.

"It's a very flexible and powerful integrated circuit, that has a couple countdown buffers and a flip-flop on the output. The electrical flip-flop circuitry on the output creates a ..."

Janet looked at Kevin's face and raised an eyebrow.

"Go on, I've worked with buffers, registers and flip-flops before."

"The 9513 creates a square wave. The output is either high or low, five volts or zero, for example, just like a square wave. The chip is designed to flip (or flop) when the countdown buffers or registers hit zero, then it repeats with a full register count again. There is a register for the high state counts, and a register for the low state."

"I think I see where you are going."

"So what you do is this," Janet continued. "From the computer or controller, you command a different integer value into each register. The chip counts from that number down to zero at a known countdown rate then flips the output from low to high. It then counts down from the other register and flops back from high to low. By putting different values in each register, you can create a pulse-width-modulated square wave of any frequency or pulse-width you want."

"Awesome." Kevin said but his brow quickly furrowed. "Do I have to design a circuit board to mount seven of these integrated circuit 9513s on, or is there a company that makes a PC interface board with several chips already on it?"

"That could be a problem. I know you can get a PC expansion board that will mount on a PC bus with five 9513s on it, but I don't know about seven."

"Five is kind of an odd number," Kevin said.

"You could buy two boards." Janet scrolled through the options in the catalog. "Do you need to control all seven motors at the same time, simultaneously?"

"Of course."

"Okay then. Let's search for boards that have multiple counter..."

"Wait." Kevin thought out loud. "The reason to have these motors is to quickly reshape the cutter and shorten the batch change time. I expect the batch change to be about a minute or two while the label rolls are changed."

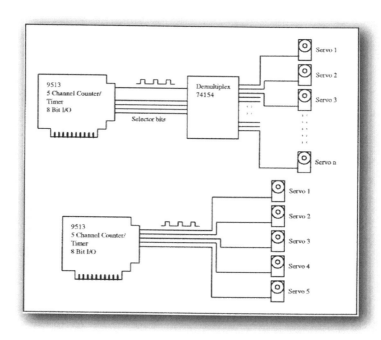

"A minute is a long time," Janet said. "Why don't you use one 9513 and a multiplexer?"

Kevin looked at Janet. His eyes moved back and forth as he mumbled the word, 'multiplexer.' He then nodded.

Janet continued, "Send one PWM signal sequentially through the multiplexer to one of the seven motors at a time, one right after the other. The 9513 chip even has several digital output signals you can command from the computer that can be used as selector bits to switch the demultiplexer." Janet typed on her keyboard again. "Here it is, 75154 demultiplexer." Janet drew a diagram showing the signal paths from the 9513 to the 75154 and on to each servomotor. "Do you think this will work?"

"I don't see why not." Kevin said. "There might be a problem pushing and pulling on the flexible blade with just one motor at a time, creating high bending moments in the blade and high forces in the rod."

Kevin tapped his pencil on his notepad. "But I suppose we could sequentially reposition all seven motors a small distance—say 10% of the desired distance—then run through them again and again until all motors are at the final destination. A minute or two should be plenty of time to do all that."

"If it doesn't work with the multiplexing, you can purchase two 9513 boards totaling 10 counter-timers, giving you three spares."

"Thanks Janet. You've made my day."

"No problem. Just tell my manager about it before

the next salary review."

For the next couple days, Kevin and Janet worked out the details of the servomotor driver, then got the parts on order.

Kevin then turned his focus to the mathematics and software necessary to control the shape of the cutter.

"Hey Kevin." Jack leaned into his cubicle. "I heard from Janet that you've got the electronics worked out for the flexible cutter servos."

"Yes, she's pretty smart," Kevin said.

"I heard that." Janet called out from a few cubes away.

Kevin lowered his voice while continuing to write equations in his engineering notebook. Several blocks of calculations were crossed-out. A few textbooks were laid open around his desk. "She knew all about integrated circuits and how to make a controlled square-wave."

"So, it looks like you're now working on the math?" Jack observed.

"Yah. I've been doing some research and..." Kevin gritted his teeth and looked up at Jack. "Do you have time to listen to my approach?"

Jack quickly sat in the guest chair in Kevin's cube.

"Why don't we go into the conference room?" Kevin said grabbing papers, a thin metal ruler, and a couple books from his desk.

Jack closed the door while Kevin erased the whiteboard in the conference room.

"Okay, for a given label, we need to drive the seven

motors to positions that will cause the blade to take on the desired shape. Our shape is pretty simple."

Kevin drew axes for an x-y graph, then in the positive quadrant (upper right), he drew a wavy horizontal curve like the long side of the wavy ribbon. He then carefully marked seven equally spaced points along the curve using heavy dots.

"This curve represents the desired shape of our cutter blade. These points represent the seven places along the curve where the control rods are attached. Each point is exactly three-quarter inches apart along the arc of the curve, just like the pivot points that are bonded to the blade. We need to determine the Y value at each of these points because that's how far the servomotors need to move."

Jack stared at the board, pinching his chin between his thumb and forefinger.

Kevin continued.

"The first thing we need to do is approximate this desired curve with a mathematical function, then find the actuation points along that curve, the dots. Since our curve is pretty smooth and it only has one concave downward part and one concave upward part, we can estimate it with a third-order, or cubic polynomial."

Kevin then marked four points along the same curve using little squares, then wrote

$$y = a + bx + cx^2 + dx^3$$

on the board.

"Using this equation, and the coordinates of these four points," Kevin pointed at each point, "we can use simultaneous equations or vector arithmetic to determine the coefficients a, b, c, and d."

"As I recall," Jack said, "fitting a curve through four points involves determinants and inverted matrices."

"Yes, but it's a pretty straightforward mathematical procedure." Kevin patted a math-book on the table. "I'm not too worried about it. I'm sure I can write the software code for that part."

This time Kevin pointed at a textbook on the table titled, Numerical Methods.

"Now, in order to move each servo to the right position, we need to know what the X and Y values are at each control point or pivot block on the blade."

"Why do you need to know the X values?"

"Well, you're right. All I really need is the Y value for each actuator."

Jack stood up and walked to the board. "You already know that each actuator is three-quarters of an inch apart along the x-axis."

Kevin shook his head but listened as Jack continued. "Why can't you just plug those X values into the new polynomial and use the resulting Y value at each of those points?"

Kevin picked up the ruler and flexed it. "Because when the spline bends, the attach points are no longer at the same spacing in the X direction, along the x-axis, that they were when the spline was flat. When the spline is flexed and bent, the actuation points are actually a little closer when projected on the x-axis."

Kevin waited for Jack's response, flexed the ruler again, then pointed it at Jack.

"I get it." Jack said. "So what's your problem?"

Kevin picked up his calculus book and held it to his chest. "The relationship between distance along a curve and x-y coordinates along the curve is given by the classical arc-length formula." (classical refers to the time period)

"Then use that formula," Jack said.

"The problem is, the formula gives the arc length as a function of incremental changes in X and Y along the curve. It's an integral where arc length

$$L = \int (ds)$$

and ds is a function of X and Y."

"I still don't see your problem. You know how to use calculus."

"For my problem, I need the opposite. I need incremental changes in X or Y given a specified arc length. I need to invert or solve this complicated equation for X and Y. It has the Pythagorean theorem in it. Integrating one over the square root of something is difficult."

"That could be a problem. You better dig into your calculus book some more and see how complicated it is to invert the arc-length formula."

"I've been searching. I've been on the internet searching university websites looking for course notes and other papers where mathematicians may have solved this problem."

The room fell silent as Kevin and Jack studied the board and thumbed through textbooks. Jack looked through the table of contents of Numerical Methods.

"Look. During a batch change, we have plenty of time to perform calculations. Can't you use a trial and error approach, an iterative method or find the roots of the equation or something like that?"

"Hm." Kevin thought for a moment. "Well, I could estimate the X value, plug it into the arc-length formula and get the approximate length, then if it's too big, I'll reduce X and try it again."

"That's what I'm talk'n about. Write a routine to solve for X."

Kevin pressed his lips together. "I'd rather have a more direct calculation to keep the software simple."

"Okay," Jack said, "but I know you're pretty good with software programming so..."

"If there isn't a closed-form solution, then I'll write an iterative routine to solve for each X given each arc L."

"I'm impressed with your determination. Or is it stubbornness?"

"Finally." Kevin held the small servomotor in his hand and pointed at the output disc. "Since each actuator has a rotary output, we need to convert from linear distance Y to rotational angle θ (theta) The software is actually required to command the angle θ. A simple trigonometry relationship will work."

Kevin wrote

$$\delta y = R\ sin(\theta)$$

on the board, and then solving for θ, he wrote

$$\theta = sin^{-1}\ (\delta y/R).$$

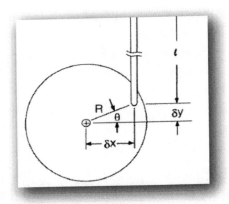

"I recognize that equation," Jack said. "I'm impressed. Now, I've been wondering. What language do you plan to write the software in?"

"Oh don't worry about that. I'm comfortable in all the latest codes."

"I confess," Jack said. "Between your math, software, and science expertise, oh, and music, and Janet's electrical engineering, I'm excited to see, and hear, the blade tapping away at the labels moving through my, I mean our machine."

For days, Kevin worked diligently on the software, running numerous test cases and making adjustments to optimize the cutter shape, making it as close to the desired ribbon shape as possible.

A few weeks later, at the ribbon cutting ceremony for the new machine, Jack, Janet, and Kevin received small gifts, and certificates of appreciation. In the upper corner of each certificate was placed a ribbon label, cut from the very machine they created. On each ribbon was written, "A cut above the rest."

Mentor Discussion and Exercises

In The Ribbon Cutting, three engineers cooperated to create an amazing machine that would automatically cut curved shapes between scrapbook shapes. Kevin, Janet, and Jack are just like real product development or industrial engineers working together to solve challenging and important problems.

1. Did you notice any differences in personality between these three engineers?
2. What about differences in academic training?
3. Was this diversity a good or a bad thing?
4. How productive would Kevin have been had he worked in isolation?
5. What contributions did Janet and Jack make?

Engineers are often faced with difficult problems to

solve. Kevin took some time to enjoy his favorite musical instrument, enjoying the art of music to rest his mind.

6. How did his love of music and art play a role in finding an engineering solution?
7. Can you think of other things in the world around us that have multiple motors or actuators packed into tight spaces?
8. How would you have solved the problem of driving a flexible spline commanded by a computer?
9. Sketch your potential solutions?
10. Can you think of a non-electric motor solution?
11. Is there a pneumatic, hydraulic, or chemical solution?
12. How did Kevin communicate his solution to Jack?

In order to select the right motor size, Kevin needed to address the science of the device. He had to determine the forces and stresses on the flexible blade and on the push rods to make sure they didn't break or buckle. He looked around and drew upon his knowledge of hobby servomotors to select something that would work for the prototype machine.

13. What problem was Kevin trying to solve when he spoke to Janet, the Electrical Engineer?

Even though Kevin had fundamental training in electrical engineering principles, Janet had more depth and background because of her training and experience (and her hobbies). The method they needed to create multiple square waves was not obvious to either engineer at first, but by looking around at other equipment, Janet reflected on how things might work and was able to consider new potential solutions.

To write the software code for the flexible cutter, Kevin needed to understand mathematics, specifically, algebra, trigonometry, and even calculus.

14. Did he have to remember everything he learned in school? What did Kevin use to help him remember his academic training?
15. Where did he look for solutions? Who did he talk to?

Mathematics is an important tool for the engineer. If a math problem seems hard, you will want to promptly ask for help, either as a student, or engineer like Kevin did in asking Jack to listen while he talked through his problem or solution.

Finally, learn to sketch. Learn to draw and communicate your ideas on paper, on the whiteboard, on the computer, or on your digital device. Having the ability to draw, draws others toward your abilities and promotes even more ideas and creativity.

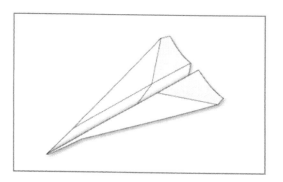

8 - MY JOURNEY TO ENGINEERING

Part 1 - Toddling and Tinkering

"We have to watch him constantly... He takes things apart and puts them back together, turns knobs and pushes buttons, and mimics the other kids..." Such was my mothers account of my first years of life experimenting with my new world, discovering how things work.

Dear reader, what was it that drew you, as a child, toward science, technology, engineering, or math?

I was born at the end of the 1950s in Burbank, California. I was a big boy, being 3 weeks late, I weighed 11 lbs, 8 oz. I shared the title of 'new arrival' with a big upright freezer which was standing by the Christmas tree when mom and I came home from the hospital. I was a child in the 1960s, a time of amazing drive and development; Apollo, jumbo jets, Supersonic Transport, to name a few. But my world was much smaller at the time.

What characteristics did I exhibit those first few years; where was my interest? My mother continued, "He would move anything that could move. At the age of two, Kenny was such a busy little guy, turning things on and off, like the water taps."

Why did I do this? Was I fascinated with water itself, or just thirsty; did I like to see the water magically appear at the turn of the handle or disappear down the mysterious hole; or was it the sound made as water expelled from the faucet or the predictable motion as it swirled down the drain?

As a minor I learned about material properties. Stingray bicycles were popular with banana seat and high handlebars. I became very proficient riding down our slightly inclined road with no hands. I was demonstrating this skill to my friends one day oblivious to the parked car in my path. I hit the car and received bruises to body and ego. Like a bowling ball plowing through two remaining pins for a spare, my two handlebars were no match for the kinetic energy of my body; they sheared right of—Did you know that welded soft-metal handlebars are never as good as the original? And who did the welding? My dad.

My dad was a handyman, my mom was busy with

handicrafts; both were very service minded. My father made cabinets and furniture for a living. I enjoyed visiting his shop, examining the machines and tools, and learning how to read blueprints (architectural drawings). On occasion dad would take me with him to help him measure a job. I became very comfortable with hammer, measuring tape, chalk-line, and basic carpenter tools. As a cub scout I made a small catapult; when at home, I worked on my tree house. My dad taught me how to work. Thanks Mom and Dad for a great start. Such are the clues that may have steered me toward engineering...

Part 2 - Drafting to Engineering

I was ten and a half years old when Neil Armstrong stepped onto the lunar dust and into the history books. Wow, I thought, looking up that evening at the moon, half illuminated by the setting sun, how amazing is that? My childhood thoughts of "The Man in the Moon" were changed forever to, "Men *on* the moon."

At my dad's work back on earth, they manufactured wood panel products with routed or grooved patterns on the panel surface. They had an automated machine that held the panel upright while a vertically and horizontally moving, two-axis router would carve a design based on data from a punched tape and tape reader (yes, a punched tape; remember this was the 60s and 70s). On one occasion, they were having trouble getting the plunge axis to work. This axis would thrust or retract the router blade into or away from the panel. If the router did not plunge or retract correctly, it would carve where it shouldn't or it would miss carving where it should have carved. If this happened, they would have to scrap the panel at some expense. They invited me, the managers 11-year-old son, to assist the machine by making sure that when it was supposed to plunge, that it did, and that when it was supposed to retract, that it did. I stood in sawdust close to the machine and watched a light on the computer or tape reader and if the router did not retract, I would grab a bar and pull it out and vice versa. The workers labeled me, 'The Automated In and Out.' Even though faulty, I thought that machine was amazing.

After routing some of their products, they covered them with thin decorative vinyl by coating the wood surface with adhesive, then vacuum-applying the plastic to the panels or other furniture (In the 30s and 40s, wood-grain vinyl was also used on cars called Woodies - before my time). In some cases this furniture vinyl plastic became a hinge for folding mitered panels into a box shape. How ingenious; how clever. (Searching the internet, I found an old newspaper article on the company; Sculptured Wood Products.)

I enjoyed math, wood & metal shop, photography, guitar, hiking, skiing, and backpacking. I even used my mom's sewing machine to make my own backpack from a kit. The backpack was nice, but I was more fascinated with the gears and shafts inside the sewing machine (I removed the top when my mom wasn't looking). In shop I made a model sailboat, a footstool, a gavel, a book shelf and a cedar chest. In photography, I enjoyed the creative artistic aspects of photo composition as well as chemical development of film and paper. I had a darkroom and equipment for developing black and white film and paper. I took my camera hiking, skiing, and to most activities.

Before the days of portable stereos, I built a wooden box and mounted an old 8-Track car stereo inside, with power supply and speakers and took it on outings with friends (No vinyl on this one). I enjoyed basic electrical wiring.

During high school, I took drafting every year. I enjoyed it; my mechanical pencil was cool. I enjoyed drawing mechanical objects and architectural structures and renderings. I thought I was pretty good at it and for a time wanted to become an architect. Working for my father over the years gave me lots of exposure to drawings, cabinetry, and construction sites; however, as I worked on wood products, I seemed more interested in the machines than in the items being built by them.

At the university I toured campus, talked to professors, and took aptitude tests. I narrowed it down to Communications and Engineering. No one in my immediate family was an engineer but it was drawing me in. Engineering seemed more practical and interesting because I wanted to design mechanisms and machines. I declared my major as Mechanical Engineering. I loved statics, dynamics, and kinematics. I would come home from numerical methods class and program the days learning into my Atari 800 (a personal computer with a whopping 16 kilobytes of RAM memory, no flash memory and no disc drive. I used a magnetic cassette tape to store my programs) I was proud of my accomplishments.

After a little research (before the internet and search engines) I figured out how to reprogram my computers' joystick port for 'output' and used it to control a little electric motor I took from an old printer.

During college I continue to work for my dad. He allowed me (with little or no budget) to build a few simple gadgets and machines to help production. While cutting or assembling a thousand drawers for hotel-room dressers and night stands, my mind was always on efficiency, "How can this job be done faster and more accurate?" I even explored books on Operations Research and the classical "Cutting Stock" problem so I could write software to help decide how to get the most out of a sheet of plywood.

Yes, I was drawn to engineering and my mind was always solving problems. I enjoyed the challenge and I couldn't wait to graduate and go to work as a real engineer.

Part 3 - From College to Industry

"What are these photos you brought?" The interviewer asked during my senior year at the university. I was applying for my first engineering job and I brought pictures of the devices I had made for my dad's cabinet shop. I think it was the photos that convinced the interviewer that I had good practical hands-on engineering experience. I got the job. We packed up our little household and moved to California, or should I say 'returned to California,' the place of my birth.

My assignment? Design and test supporting structures for satellite payloads. Requirements? High strength to weight ratios with high reliability. I learned about space environments, material properties, computer aided design systems, and how aerospace companies work.

After a couple years I became a test engineer, then system safety analyst, then electronics packaging designer, then... Each assignment gave me experience in new areas of engineering. I tried diligently to learn company goals and objectives and participate in process improvement initiatives. This focus brought trust and new opportunities to serve and grow. But I wasn't finished with school yet. I wanted a masters degree and I wanted to continue my education; I loved to learn.

I applied for graduate school, was accepted and returned to the university.

I was in tears as I left the math building one warm June day. Summer on college campus was relatively quiet, but my mind was clamoring with the noise of theorems and derivations, and proofs drumming away at my confidence. "What have I gotten myself into?" I thought. I had left a good paying job and returned to college after nine years to pursue a master of science degree in mechanical engineering. The very first class I had was Linear Algebra. It was a lot of work relearning matrices and vectors, moving into linear transformations, determinants, eigenvalues and all their applications. There were times when I didn't know if I could do it, but I kept at it and looked for ways each day to apply my new knowledge so that it would be interesting and meaningful. How meaningful could Linear Algebra be?

Do you remember the other day when you played a video game, or went to an animated digital movie. How did the movie makers make those complex graphic images look so convincing and real? Perhaps just today you swiped your fingers on a touch pad or touch screen and the photograph you just captured moved or rotated or zoomed at your command. Chances are pretty good that the people who programmed your device used linear algebra or matrix arithmetic to pan, zoom, scale, rotate, or even give depth perspective and reflection to the scene making it look real, like you were really there.

If you think of each point or pixel on the screen as a member of a large array or matrix of vectors ($\nearrow$: lines with magnitude and direction), then using the rules or theorems of linear algebra you can program all these points to move or change color or take on different shades of grey or even reflect light coming from another point (a.k.a., ray tracing). You can even make one object appear to disappear behind the one in front of it (It's called "hidden line or object removal"). It's pretty amazing actually. Suppose one matrix represents an object on your screen, say the eight corners of a cube, and let's say you throw the cube off a tall building, or at least you want your audience to think it is really being thrown off a building, you can use the laws of physics (classical mechanics) to calculate what a real cube would do as it falls (speed, rotation, trajectory or arc), and then multiply the cube matrix by the speed, rotation, and trajectory pipeline of matrices to get the next frame of the movie, update the pixels on the screen and then repeat the process over and over again forty times per second until the cube hits the ground. But wait, don't stop there, you can continue the scene as the cube bounces or crushes, or gets stepped on...

Linear Algebra is used in computer graphics, games, chemistry, flying real airplanes, economics, forecasting the weather, data compression (e.g. JPEG), sociology, traffic flow, electrical circuits, and many many other applications.

During my graduate work, and after, I have used Linear Algebra to write my own computer graphics software, develop mechanical systems to reshape complex surfaces, and many other things. When I create using a computer aided design (CAD) application, I understand what the software is doing when I click the mouse or drag a feature from one point to another. When I sit down to a digitally animated movie, I'm a little distracted from the story because "I know how they do it!" I know how they made all those characters move around and do what they do. Linear Algebra is a powerful tool. No tears anymore, just determination. I still don't have all the rules memorized; but that's okay, they're not hidden. I know where to find them. (Keep your textbooks)

In graduate school I took Linear Algebra, finite element method, CAD software development, and utilized these tools in my thesis to research numerical-to-physical surface shape manipulation. I wanted to morph surfaces; surfaces that could be used as forms to shape other objects. I applied for funding and built numerically controlled surfaces (See Engineering Story "The Ribbon Cutting" for a fictionalized story based on my thesis). While the academics were fresh in mind, I took the professional engineering exam and received my license to make sure doors of opportunity were always open.

Following graduate school, I worked in industrial automation designing new methods to handle printed circuit boards during production (See fictionalized Engineering Story "Get A Grip"). I also worked as an Engineering Manager during those years. I think the master of science degree was an advantage in my career. Eventually I returned to the aerospace world with modeling and simulation work on guidance, navigation, and control instruments. Along the way I developed my writing skills, a plus that opened more and more opportunities.

I have also looked for opportunities to serve as a mentor to other young engineers; another investment with definite returns. Although not my motive, I was always improved, when I sought to improve and help others. Several stories in this book, for example, are based on experiences gained while coaching and mentoring engineering college seniors.

Such has been my satisfying journey to and through engineering. What will your journey be like?

SYNOPSIS OF EACH STORY

In **Get a Grip**, a young engineer is astonished to be assigned to an experienced team responsible for developing critical automation in the manufacture of smart phones. She travels with the team on a foreign customer visit, participates in creative concept generation, and helps the team through difficult setbacks and technical problems.

In **The Orbital Mechanic**, a solar flare knocks a space probe off course endangering a costly mission. A simple solution comes just in time from an unlikely source to save the spacecraft. In this story, learn how engineers use science, math and physics to get spaceships from Earth out to distant planets and beyond.

In **Foot Notes**, an engineer is faced with the daunting task of inventing a cost effective foot scanner in a short amount of time, driven to search for and consider possible solutions, taking clues from the near and far, the past and present, the people and objects all around. After much effort, old impractical perceptions are pushed aside by new achievable techniques.

In **Quick Step**, an engineering team is required to create a way to make customer arch supports (orthotics) in 30 minutes. They face hurdle after hurdle as they try to find an answer to a fundamental friction problem. In the end, after much frustration, determination and creativity, they stumble onto a completely different yet very elegant approach.

In **Cutting Edge**, a student engineering team wins a bid to develop an automated synthetic diamond cleaning (blasting) machine. They familiarize and immerse themselves in customer needs, write specifications, research similar equipment, brainstorm solutions and evaluate their options. They experience the pain of unforeseen problems and the thrill of success looking externally and internally to find answers to complex questions.

In **Speed Reader**, two engineers have been working hard for weeks to prepare for and demonstrate the capability of their design. On the Friday of their last week of testing, the customer is not fully satisfied, launching the engineers into a last minute creative mode to find a quick and reliable solution, and to save their weekend plans.

In **The Ribbon Cutting**, three engineers work to create a complex system, a cutting machine with a blade that automatically morphs into shapes needed for unique products. Ideas and solutions are found all around them, in their hobbies, in other machines, in books and online. Their specific talents unite as they help each other move their company forward.

Use the following search phrase online to find additional Engineering Stories.

"Hardman" AND "Engineering Stories"

ABOUT THE AUTHOR

Ken Hardman graduated from Brigham Young University with a Master of Science degree in Mechanical Engineering. He is an Associate Technical Fellow at a major aerospace company, and a Licensed Professional Engineer. As of this writing, he has worked nearly 30 years in the aerospace and industrial automation fields defining, creating, researching, evaluating, managing, testing, and supporting satellites, aircraft, test equipment, and industrial automation. As an Adjunct Faculty, Ken has mentored and coached engineering students for many of those years. He loves to solve design problems, create useful solutions and encourage others to do the same.

Made in the USA
Lexington, KY
11 June 2015